THE RISING LEGACY

THE RISING LEGACY

LEGACY OF THE SHADOW'S BLOOD™ BOOK 3

E.G. BATEMAN

MICHAEL ANDERLE

LMBPN Publishing
PMB 196, 2540 South Maryland Pkwy
Las Vegas, NV 89109

First US edition, September 2020
(Originally published as a part of Legacy of the Shadow's Blood)
eBook ISBN: 978-1-64971-162-5
Print ISBN: 978-1-64971-163-2

THE RISING LEGACY TEAM

Thanks to our Beta Readers:

Erika Everest, Nicole Emens, Jim Caplan, Mary Morris, John Ashmore, Kelly O'Donnell, Larry Omans, Michael Baumann

Thanks to our JIT Team:

Dave Hicks
Deb Mader
Debi Sateren
Diane L. Smith
Dorothy Lloyd
Erika Everest
Jackey Hankard-Brodie
James Caplan
Jeff Eaton
Jeff Goode
John Ashmore
Lori Hendricks
Micky Cocker

Misty Roa
Paul Westman
Peter Manis
Rachel Beckford
Veronica Stephan-Miller

Editor
SkyHunter Editing Team

DEDICATIONS

Phil, for not only believing in me, but for hopping aboard this crazy train.
Michael Anderle, for your support, mentorship and above all, patience.
Craig Martelle, for being an inspiration and providing a place for me and so many others to grow as authors.
Erika Everest, Kate Pickford, Anne Lown, Natalie Roberts and Charles Tillman - For your support, time and kindness.
And… for the readers, always for you.

— E.G. Bateman

To Family, Friends and
Those Who Love
To Read.
May We All Enjoy Grace
To Live The Life We Are
Called.

— Michael Anderle

CHAPTER ONE

"*Alexa, Alexa, I hope a witch'll hex ya.*"

"*Alicia, Alicia, I'm not gonna miss ya.*"

"*Will you two knock it off? Don't make me come up there.*"

Lexi's eyes snapped open. The world spun and her vision was blurred. She closed her eyes again for a few seconds, then opened them slowly and blinked to try to clear them. An unfamiliar room slipped in and out of focus. She stretched on a couch and a face loomed above her, but it was too blurry to identify.

"She's waking up."

That voice. I should know it.

As she shook her head slightly, the face began to clear. The dark hair and olive skin were familiar, as were his brown eyes. The stubble was new, though, and her hand moved as if of its own volition to touch it. "Bryan?"

"Hi, Lexi-Loo." He smiled at her but moved beyond her reach.

She startled when she heard the nickname he used to call her and withdrew her hand. A few moments later, her surroundings settled and her vision cleared.

Briefly, she wondered if she was in a dream, but common

sense told her she couldn't invent this adult version of his face. "You were bitten by a shifter. They shot you."

He nodded. "With a dart gun. I remember."

When she tried to sit, the dizziness returned, so she gave up the effort and stared at him.

Dick's voice spoke from behind them. "You must have been what, fifteen? I didn't think they let mages out to chase shifters at that age."

Bryan turned to speak over the couch she lay on. "I wasn't supposed to be there. The family had been called out while I was with them. I think we were on the way back from a restaurant."

Lexi closed her eyes again. "It was Maggie's birthday." She smiled as a memory came to her. "Isaac hung a birthday banner across the living room, but he attached it using his little cross-bolt gun and fired it into the corners of the room. Dad went nuts and the dinner was almost canceled." She remembered the restaurant. Her Kindred sister, Maggie, had blown out seventeen candles on her cake.

Her Kindred brother chuckled. "I'd forgotten about that. Lexi had only just started going out on jobs with the family. I was supposed to stay in the car, but I was bored and fifteen and thought I'd be able to watch the action from a safe distance. While they were looking for the shifter, he had escaped from a window and surprised me. I couldn't make an energy ball yet, but I managed to shock him enough to make him run off.

"The family didn't realize I'd been bitten. I'd healed the wound before they returned to the car because I was more afraid of being grounded than dying. Within hours, I had a fever and started hallucinating. I remembered events I swore had happened but no one else seemed to recall them."

She opened her eyes to look at him again. "When they realized you'd been bitten, I was forbidden to go near you, but they couldn't keep us apart. We did everything together. I'd climbed in the window and found you covered in sweat and shivering. Then, after a few days of you raving, a Kindred unit came from another city. Some cold-faced bitch pulled me out of the room, and I heard shouting.

"Braxton argued with them, then I heard the shot. I thought it was from a silenced weapon. I tried to break away from the woman, but she counseled me. She took the memories away—not only of that event, but it was as though you had never existed until Barry the vampire tried to turn me. I tasted vampire blood and the memories tumbled back." Still gazing at him, she asked. "Have you always remembered?"

He paused for a moment before he responded. "Yes."

Still befuddled, she tried to process it. Her memories of him had only returned a year before and she had thought he was dead. But he had always known he'd left her behind. It hurt that he'd never made contact.

Her eyes stung at the thought and she dragged her gaze away from him. The blinds were closed and she couldn't get a sense of where they were. "How long have I been out? Where are we?"

"You've been out a few hours. We're in North Carolina." Dolores appeared from behind the couch. She put a cup of coffee on the table in front of her before she walked out of sight again. Lexi looked at the cup. It was one she had bought Dolores and said *I'm Tired Of Adulting. Let's Be Fairies.*

The others seemed to be giving her and Bryan a little space, but she could feel a swell of emotions from Scott. They were all hopelessly entwined with her feelings and she wasn't sure who felt what or even that she had the energy to sift through them.

She looked at Bryan. "Where is she?" She didn't have to say who she meant. Everyone would know she was talking about the sister she'd only recently discovered existed.

He frowned and scraped his mop of dark hair away from his face. "Back in New Orleans, at Dad's place."

"Dad?" Her heart raced. Had Alicia been living with their parents?

Bryan seemed to know where her thoughts had jumped to. "Our Kindred unit leader—Kevin Rand, the police chief. Not her real dad."

"The chief's your dad? The man who gave Lorenzo the go-ahead to murder all those people? How are you okay with that?" Lexi was shocked.

"I'm not okay with it. Dad wouldn't be either. Not that it matters. He had one of his weird phone calls from Caleb. I've seen him when it happens. The man calls and starts speaking, his face goes blank, and there are things he doesn't remember. It's different than counseling. I don't know how Caleb does it." Bryan shrugged. "As far as Kevin knows, Lorenzo went crazy. I told him she'd fought him and killed him."

"Kindred saves us all again, woohoo!" Dick's voice, still from behind, dripped with sarcasm.

Bryan looked up, presumably at the vampire, and shrugged apologetically. "She collapsed after your fight. I counseled her before she woke up again. Dad's not happy about that and it's against Kindred procedures. I don't like counseling her but it's the only way I could think to cover your trail and give me space in which to get answers. I already suspected you were involved as the hotel staff in Cabo were adamant that Ali had been there for over a week."

Dolores spoke from where she presumably waited with Dick. "Didn't they counsel you?"

"Not yet, but the memories always come back anyway. They don't know that."

Lexi nodded. "Because of the shifter bite."

His brows drew together in puzzlement. "No."

"No?" She frowned at him in confusion. "But I thought that was why they shot you—because the counseling stopped working and you remembered things they were trying to hide."

Bryan nodded his understanding. "You're kind of right. If we're tainted by a sting, bite, or the blood of a supernatural, counseling might not work for a while until we're fully healed. Then, usually, everything goes back to normal."

"I didn't know," she responded, still a little confused. "It was one of the reasons I ran from them. I thought they might realize I'd been tainted by the vampire blood and call someone in to kill me."

"Tainted? Excuse me, I'm right here." Dick sounded offended.

Bryan looked up. "Sorry, that's a Kindred term."

"Quelle Surprise," the vampire muttered.

She watched her once-brother while he spoke. He'd grown into a handsome man. She twisted her mother's wedding ring.

He looked at the ring and smiled. "You still have that."

Lexi smiled when she looked at the band. "It's always meant a lot to me but I never knew why. When they took the memory of you, I also lost the memory I would have had if I'd found out it had belonged to my mother."

Bryan returned his gaze to her face. "Dolores told me about the vamp trying to turn you. Is that when you started to remember me?" He waited for her to confirm with a nod, then tilted his head with a curious expression. "But that's only one of the reasons why you ran. You thought they'd murdered me. What else?"

"We'd been on a job. A kid had been kidnapped by a vampire —the one who tried to turn me. We rescued the boy and he was supposed to go back to his parents. They counseled us the next morning after I'd submitted my report but it didn't work on me. I was scared so I didn't tell anyone. Later, they counseled us again and implanted the existence of a little brother called Bobby. It almost worked and for a brief moment, I totally believed it. When he walked in, though, I recognized him instantly as the kid who'd been kidnapped. They hadn't taken him to his parents. He had mage potential so they kept him." She shook her head. "His poor parents."

"It sounds like the taint—uh, the vampire blood was wearing

off and counseling was starting to work again. But then they introduced the kid who was already in your memory. The moment you saw him, it caused a conflict. Your brain rejected the new information."

Lexi felt confused by it all. "So they don't kill people who have been tainted—I mean…uh, contaminated. Sorry, Dick, that's not any better, is it?"

The vampire sighed dramatically.

Bryan shook his head. "You mean the horror stories we heard growing up? Sometimes. If that vampire had succeeded in turning you, they would have eliminated you."

She nodded. "Or if the shifter had turned you back then."

"Exactly."

That triggered her recall of something she'd been curious about. "That reminds me, what attacked Alicia? Those marks on her face."

He paused and gnawed his lip before he answered. "Yes, that was a werewolf."

After a niggle of guilt, she chastised herself mentally for being so blunt. "I'm sorry. Did you kill it?"

"I tried." He looked away.

Lexi narrowed her eyes. "It was you, wasn't it?"

His mouth opened but he didn't say anything.

While she knew he knew what she meant, she said it anyway. "In the street, when we were with Thomas and Lorenzo attacked us. It was you who saved us."

"Er… Yes. Joseph had told me about you."

"I wish he'd done me the same courtesy." She lowered her head carefully. "So, I have a sister and I almost killed her."

Bryan put his hand on her arm. "She won't remember it."

For a moment, at his touch, memories and feelings flowed through her like a tidal wave, followed immediately by a feeling of jealousy and hurt that came from Scott.

She did her best to push Scott's feelings away, not because she didn't care but because it was all too much. "But I remember it. I don't know what got into me."

"It was probably something residual from the ring," Dolores said, still out of sight. Bryan looked up and Lexi had a feeling they shared some unspoken concern.

Without thought, she rubbed her face where Alicia had punched her. It didn't hurt, obviously. Scott would have seen to that.

Bryan looked at her again. "Do you remember anything about Alicia? Have any old memories resurfaced?"

"No." She thought about the dream she'd had—two little girls teasing each other—but it had been fleeting and was already drifting away. "I didn't know I had a sister until you came into that room and stopped me from taking her head off."

He raised an eyebrow. "Well, thank you for stopping. Look, I'll tell you what I know, but it's not much."

"I think I need to sit for this." Lexi swung her legs to the floor and pushed into a seated position. She caught a glimpse of Scott, Dick, and Dolores at a table behind the couch. Scott was the only one who didn't return her gaze. He stared resolutely ahead.

God knows what must be going through his mind.

Bryan continued. "I only know what I've overheard and it's not much. When you were six, a decision was made to separate you and you were taken to different Kindred families."

"What about our real parents? Were they Kindred? Or were we kidnapped like Bobby?"

"I don't know about that. I'm sorry, but Ali is unusual. She's the strongest and fastest legacy I've ever seen."

His words hurt although she knew he hadn't intended that. He would remember that she was almost a complete dud. She covered her discomfort by rubbing her jaw again. "I noticed that."

She thought about the fight with her sister and how she'd seemed stronger than might have been believed, and how at the end, she had sagged. "Right now, I feel weaker than I've ever felt in my life."

Dick cleared his throat. "It's understandable. She slapped you into next week."

Lexi twisted in her seat and leveled a gaze at him. He sat at the table facing her and shrugged. "Well, she did."

She turned to Bryan. "Can I meet her?"

"Rematch?" the vampire muttered.

"Are you for real?" Her glare didn't seem to have much effect.

Dick raised an eyebrow. "What? You broke my neck. I can't experience a little schadenfreude?"

Bryan spoke quickly. "I don't want to put her in danger. Also, it would be awkward because she doesn't know I remember things. I've told her things before, but she didn't take it well and I had to counsel her. I hate doing that."

Lexi knew she had to ask her next question as dispassionately as possible, but she couldn't do it looking into his eyes. She picked the mug of coffee up and stared into it. "She's your wife, isn't she?"

"Yes." His voice was soft

While she tried to remain nonchalant and managed to swallow the lump in her throat, it seemed loud as though it were a rock. She grimaced, sure the whole room had heard it. Again, a swell of pity came through the empathetic link.

She silently tested the question she wanted to ask but couldn't because it was stupid and pointless. *Why did they take you away from me and give you to her?*

Lexi felt like she was fifteen again and the pain of losing Bryan was still raw from her core to her fingertips.

With a slow, deliberate movement, she put the mug down. It was time to regain control of herself. "Is Broullard okay? The chief and Caleb were going to—"

Bryan shook his head. "He's fine. I counseled him before I came here and he won't remember any of you."

Dick sighed. "Charles won't remember me? That makes me sad."

Lexi understood how he felt. She liked Broullard too.

"I told the chief I'd done it," Bryan continued. "They'll leave him alone—"

"You can't assume that," Lexi interrupted. "Caleb wanted him dead and he has a very long arm."

"He's safe for now. I don't know what else I can do." He shrugged as though helping the detective was truly beyond him.

She stood. "Counsel him again. Tell him to retire on medical grounds. Send him on a cruise. Get him out of there."

He put his hands on her arms. "You're right. I'll do what I can."

The move shocked her. For a fraction of a second, she thought of either kissing him or head-butting him.

Bryan seemed to sense the conflict and stepped back.

Lexi sat again. "I assume you know all about Caleb now."

"We told him," Scott said.

Her Kindred brother picked a glass of water up and took a sip. "I've had suspicions about him for a while. I've met him a few times, but they always counsel me after, thinking they can make me forget him. Still, there isn't much I can tell you. It sounds like you all know a hell of a lot more about him than I've gleaned.

"I've overheard Dad talk about him having business interests in South Africa. But more recently, he purchased a business on behalf of Kindred in Maine. I don't know the details, only that it was some kind of hostile takeover and he's in the process of changing the management team. There isn't much I can do to help you without putting Alicia in danger."

She was annoyed and felt the situation deserved to be taken more seriously. "Why not? Surely Caleb's a risk to everyone. I assume they've told you he's trying to bring a particularly powerful high-level demon into our world."

"I don't know who else is involved. If we show our hand now

and discover the whole council is conspiring with him, we're dead. I know for a fact he's been practicing outlawed magic."

"I know that. I killed his doppelgänger, remember? That ritual takes thirteen members—or proxies like your dad. Yes, we noticed your dad's lost twenty percent of his fingers."

"Precisely. The council is thirteen. What if it's all of them? I might be able to get some information out of Kevin, although it wouldn't surprise me if Caleb counsels him each time they go to meetings together. That happens at least once a month."

Lexi straightened. "That works perfectly. We could find out where they meet and stick something pointy between his ribs."

Bryan looked doubtfully at her. "You don't look like you could poke him in the ribs with a finger. Maybe you need to get your strength back. I'll keep my eyes and ears open and let you know anything I learn, but I'm not sure this is even your problem, is it? You left Kindred."

She raked her fingers through her hair. "Like I said, this is everyone's problem. If I thought I could trust Kindred to deal with their own mess, I would because honestly, I think this will be the death of us."

He moved her mug and sat on the wooden table in front of her. "Lexi, I have to ask this. Did you do anything to Alicia? Anything magical?"

The memory of the fight resurfaced and she put her hands over her face and shook her head. "I almost pulverized her but no, nothing magical. Why?"

"We're keeping her sedated because she had aggression issues. When she initially woke, she threw her mom across the room so hard, it would have killed a normal person. Luckily, her mom was able to translocate out. Then, she punched her way through a metal door. She was feral. When I scanned her body, the density of her bones had doubled. That can't suddenly happen by itself."

Lexi felt the accusation in the air. She leveled her gaze at him.

"I said I didn't do anything like that. Scott and I have only been matched for a few months. I'm still learning."

Bryan held a hand up. "That's fine, I believe you. I merely need to look harder for an answer, that's all." He sighed and looked at her. "I didn't think I'd ever see you again, Lexi-Loo."

She looked away, feeling awkward. "I thought *you* were dead so I doubt you're as surprised as I am." She looked back at him. "Why did they take you away?"

He shrugged. "New Orleans is a melting pot of supernaturals. It's a huge community." He made a gun with his fingers and pretended to blow smoke off the imaginary barrel. "I guess they needed their best man." He gave her a lop-sided grin.

And their best woman.

Bryan stood. "I need to get back. Scott knows how to contact me if you need me." He vanished.

Lexi looked up and scowled at the others, who all seemed to watch her with pity in their eyes. She hated it. "So, what's next for us? I can't sit around waiting to hear from him."

"A break, then. A real one this time." Dolores patted her on the shoulder.

She shook her head. "I'd rather get back to work if it's all the same."

The woman sighed and it appeared that was the response she'd expected. "As you wish. I've had a job come in and I was going to give it to someone local to the area but honestly, there aren't many supernaturals near this one. It's in Las Vegas. A lucky talisman has been stolen."

Dick spun in his seat. "Stolen? Magical items are protected in Las Vegas. The only way to steal them would be with magic, which is impossible with the wards in place."

Dolores nodded her agreement. "I don't understand it either. Many magical items are in Las Vegas for that precise reason."

Lexi drained her mug and stood. "Surely it would have been

taken out of town immediately. Even if it were somehow stolen, I can't imagine how it could be used in Vegas."

Her boss took the mug from her. "I think you're right. If it really is gone, I hope Scott can follow it."

Dick asked the question she had intended to ask next. "Why haven't they called the local Kindred unit in for this?"

"One of the staff members at the museum is a supe," the fae explained. "An old friend who works as a historian. He did call Kindred yesterday morning when it was found to be missing, and they told him to keep looking for it. They think it's more likely someone at the museum has mislaid it. He knows that's not the case, freaked out, and called me."

Scott's brow wrinkled. "Why would a supe work somewhere they can't use all their abilities?"

Dolores continued to speak as she put the mugs and glasses into the kitchen. "He likes the dry heat."

Lexi had the feeling that wasn't the real reason, but it was none of their business. She watched as Marcel woke, yawned and stretched, and padded to Dick.

The vampire scratched the puppy's head absently. "Are Kindred sure the wards are all still in place?"

Dolores returned to the room. "They insist that no magic has been or could be performed in Las Vegas except by license."

Lexi turned to the fae. "Why is there even a Kindred unit in Las Vegas if it's so locked down?"

The woman laughed. "Because they perform twice a night on the Strip, dear."

"That figures." She stood. "At least I'll know who the local Kindred mages are. It'll be fairly easy to avoid people whose faces are plastered all over the billboards."

"So we're going. Marvelous! I wonder if Celine's performing. I'll give her a call while I walk Marcel." Dick stood and took the lead from the table. "Marcel, walkies."

He attached the lead while the puppy wagged his stumpy tail.

When he opened the door, the sudden loud cacophony of traffic sounds made Lexi jump. He turned to them. "Toodle-pip." Marcel scrambled to get through the door and Dick followed before he closed it behind them.

The room returned to silence. After a moment, she flopped like a sullen teen and rolled her eyes. "Does he have to come?"

Dolores's eyebrows raised in surprise. "Don't you want him on the team?"

Lexi tutted. "No… Yes… He's so annoying."

The fae patted her cheek. "You can be annoying too, dear."

She exhaled sharply. "That's what he says. Okay, fine, but only because I've grown attached to Marcel."

CHAPTER TWO

Lexi sat at the table next to Scott. He'd barely said a word and she placed her hand palm-up on the table beside his. He continued to stare ahead with worry lines across his forehead. After a moment, he stood and walked through the French doors at the back of the room and onto a porch.

Dolores stood behind the girl's chair and put her hands on her shoulders. "Give him time. He knows Bryan was your intended blood match and whatever feelings you have for him, Scott can feel that. He's confused."

"I know." She walked to the window and opened the blinds. It was dark but she could see a row of lights from homes dotted along the shores of a lake. The gleam from an almost full but waning moon reflected on the water. Scott walked along a small boardwalk. "I don't know what to tell him. He's not the only one who's confused, but it's not like we're a couple or anything."

"He probably wonders if you regret being matched with him now you know Bryan's still alive."

"Bryan's still alive and apparently, he's my brother-in-law. I don't think Scott has anything to worry about." She studied their surroundings curiously. "Where exactly are we?"

"Here and there." Dolores joined her at the window and pointed. "That's Lake Norman. It's about thirty miles from Charlotte."

They watched together as the sorcerer walked to the end of the boardwalk and sat with his legs crossed. Lexi glanced at her companion. "Maybe I should talk to him and apologize."

The fae remained focused on Scott. "You have nothing to apologize for. I've always felt the blood match is more curse than anything. They make you all want it so much—like you won't be complete without the never-ending agony of an unhealing scar and the weight of someone else's emotional crap for the rest of your life."

She smirked. "Well, when you put it like that…" She looked at the still water and quiet woods. "How far to the nearest coffee shop?"

"If you go out that way? About five miles. Leave by the front door instead. It opens into the middle of Charlotte and there's a Starbucks across the street."

Lexi crossed the room and opened the front door to look out. The city sounds blasted again. It was late in the evening and the traffic was still quite heavy, but she located the Starbucks sign across the street. She turned to her companion. "Okay, so what would happen if I stepped out of here and climbed over the roof? Where would I be?"

Dolores smiled. "Good luck with that."

With a grin, she strolled out. On the street, she turned and looked at the door she'd left through. Her gaze traced up the building from there and she had to crane her neck to follow its lines to the top. It was a skyscraper. Chuckling, she turned and headed across the street.

Fae magic is so cool.

She returned ten minutes later with an iced caramel latte for herself and an iced peppermint white chocolate mocha for Scott. He was still out near the water in the dark and she wandered out to join him. As soon as she opened the door, insects buzzed in the otherwise silent world.

As she approached, she noticed that he held a little energy ball in his palm. "That's nice."

He glanced at her as she settled beside him. "This will be your next lesson. No more exploding voodoo stones for you."

Lexi recalled the liquified gore that had dripped from his hair after she'd used the voodoo stone in New Orleans a few days before. It was inappropriate but she couldn't stifle a giggle.

Scott looked sharply at her before he chuckled too. "God, that was awful."

They both laughed.

She put the cupholder between them, pulled her latte out, and looked onto the water. "If it weren't for those houses over there, it would be almost completely black out here." She looked at the apartment. It was an abandoned fishing shack from the outside.

He threw the energy ball and they watched as it skipped over the water like a stone and left a trail of light before it flickered and disappeared. He picked his drink up and took a long sip of it. "So, what's it like to have a twin sister?"

Lexi thought about it, then sighed. "I think I was happier when I thought I had a doppelgänger."

The sorcerer turned to her. "You were looking for answers—"

"She's not an answer. She's a thousand more questions."

"I'm sorry for how I reacted." He returned his focus to the water. "It's confusing, feeling all those emotions coming from you."

She wasn't sure what those emotions were herself but did know he felt insecure. Talking about it seemed unfair so she decided to divert the conversation. "That goes both ways, you know."

"What do you mean?" He looked genuinely puzzled.

"You've been pining for your new fairy girlfriend since you got back from Fae." She smirked.

Scott put his drink down. "That's not fair. She's not my girlfriend. She attacked me. I have to ride it out until her compulsion wears off."

Lexi elbowed him lightly. "You mean *we* have to ride it out."

He sighed, then barked a laugh. "We're not exactly the poster kids for life after Kindred, are we?"

In response, she held her cup up. "Dude, I think we're the only examples. To the ex-Kindred fuck-up society."

"I think we do some good, though, don't you?" He bumped his cup against hers.

"No. I think we do a ton of good. I think we do great." Lexi adjusted her position so she faced him. "We're on the run from the largest supernatural organization on the planet. Are we hiding?"

Scott gave her a lop-sided grin. "A little."

"Well, okay, but we still kick ass." She held her cup up and they bumped again.

Dolores opened the door of the shack. "If you two have finished congratulating yourselves, Dick's back. Let's get to work."

They walked inside to find the vampire pulling cartons of Chinese food out of a bag. "I didn't know what you all eat so I bought a selection."

The fae looked at Lexi with her eyebrows raised in silent admonishment for her suggestion that he shouldn't be on the team.

She smiled in response and nodded as she put her coffee cup on the table. "I'm going to wash up."

Dolores pointed. "It's past the kitchen."

After the kitchen, one more door was visible along the hallway. She stepped in and washed her hands. When she joined the others at the table, she opened the box in front of her. "Orange chicken, perfect." She looked at Dick. "Thank you."

After dinner, Dolores cleared the cartons into the trash.

"Okay, you guys, I need the table for work. Go out and get some exercise."

Scott turned to Lexi and Dick. "Do you want to explore the town?"

The vampire looked out onto the water. "I'll have a little quiet time at the lake. I might catch up later."

The two young people left via the front door and walked along quiet streets for a while.

"We don't seem to be in the middle of the action, do we?" the sorcerer said when he finally stopped. He didn't wait for an answer but scrolled through his cell phone. "Right, let's move this along." He caught hold of his companion and teleported.

Lexi looked around and after a few moments, realized that they stood on the street outside a large gate. She read the sign. "Hey, a theme park."

Scott grinned. "I've always wanted to visit a theme park."

"You've never been to one?"

"Not as far as I know, but you know what it's like. I could have been to ten theme parks and they might have taken it all away. I can't believe I ever thought counseling was justified." He looked through the iron bars of the gate before he extended his arm to her. "One more hop."

She took his arm and he teleported them into the entertainment venue.

They walked along stalls which were all closed but which carried signs for popcorn, cotton candy, hook-a-duck, and hotdogs.

Finally, they stopped in front of a huge rollercoaster.

He gazed longingly at it. "Look at the size of it."

Lexi pulled him. "Let's sit in it."

They climbed easily over the gate and up to the first car, then sat in the front and clicked the safety belts.

She shook her head. "I can't believe you haven't been to a theme park. That's a tragedy. We should go to one."

Scott put his hand on the car. His lips moved and it moved a few inches, then stopped. He looked at her. "What do you think?"

"What's keeping you?" She grinned. "Fire this baby up."

The car climbed the track slowly. When it reached the top, he took his hand away and it stopped.

He looked around into the distance. "We can see for miles."

They both laughed, then fell silent. He turned to her. "I know you're thinking about him. You can talk about him. I don't mind."

Lexi thought he probably did mind, but a memory had come to her in those moments and she wanted to share it. "When Bryan was with us, we must have been around twelve. We used to climb out of the attic window and sit on the roof. While we were up there, we'd play a game called What Would You Do?"

"What's that?"

"Okay, let's give it a go. What would you do if a shifter suddenly appeared in front of you?"

Scott's brows drew down in thought. "It depends. Might it be Edward or Agatha?"

They knew shifters, so the game wouldn't be as easy as it had been when they were kids. She sighed. "Say it wasn't. For the purposes of the game, it's a bad shifter."

He grinned. "You're my legacy. I'd call you."

Lexi looked at him, her expression deadpan. "I've been knocked unconscious."

"Oh, right. I'd paralyze him until you woke up. Then you could deal with him."

She rolled her eyes. "Now you ask me one."

The sorcerer thought for a moment. "What would you do if a dark fae suddenly appeared in front of you…with malicious intent?"

Lexi nodded. "Easy. I'd take my katana out and chop her head off."

"Her?"

"You're thinking of the one who attacked you, aren't you?"

He exhaled huffily. "I guess. Although I think I could have guessed that answer."

"My turn. What would you do if Azatoth appeared in front of you?"

Immediately, he gave her a lop-sided grin. "Run like fuck."

What could she do but laugh? "Come on, then. You ask. Try to make it a hard one."

Scott chewed his lip as he thought hard. "What would you do if Dick suddenly appeared in front of you and…uh, and kissed you. With tongues."

Lexi thumped his arm and laughed. "Oh, gross. I'd break his nose."

"You wouldn't be that lucky." Dick's voice startled them.

"Christ almighty, you almost gave me a heart attack." Her hand clutched her chest.

"Don't blame me. I was on the other side of town and I suddenly appeared here as though I had been conjured."

She twisted in her seat to look at him "You're kidding!" She glanced at Scott, about to ask if he'd done it.

"Of course I'm kidding. I heard you two from half a mile away. Does this go?" Dick settled into the seat behind them and clicked the safety belt. "Safety first. Actually, I did once get my nose broken for kissing a woman. I'll tell you about it sometime."

Scott put a hand on the front of the car and it accelerated along the rails.

As the car came in toward the rear of the others, she noticed the beam from a flashlight.

"Who's there?" a gravelly voice demanded in the darkness.

Scott grabbed Lexi and Dick and teleported to the apartment.

Seconds later, they stood outside the building. The sorcerer seemed surprised and he looked around with a frown. "I aimed for the inside."

They stepped into Dolores's apartment to find she'd left a

note on the table for them. *I've turned in. Bedrooms have been prepared for you. Please lock the doors before you go to bed.*

Scott turned and locked the door as instructed.

Lexi looked around, "Where are we supposed to sleep? I didn't see any bedrooms." She looked down the hallway. It was longer than she remembered and there were now two doors she would swear she hadn't seen before beyond the bathroom. She opened the first to find it had two beds and the second had one bed and a dog basket. Marcel was already asleep on the floor next to the basket.

She returned to the others. "There are now two bedrooms that weren't here before." She shook her head and chuckled.

Dick paused at the French doors. "What are you laughing at?

"I've been around magic my whole life, but it was mostly only used to hurt or control people. Since I've worked with Dolores, I've seen the good things it can do—and the fun things."

The vampire opened the French doors. "Lexi Braxton, I do believe you've gone native. Welcome to the dark side." He wiggled his eyebrows and stepped out.

Lexi yawned. "I'm heading to bed."

Scott looked at the lake. "I'll be along soon. I'll sit with Dick for a few minutes."

She went to sleep listening to the low murmurs of the men talking.

The sorcerer was leaving the bathroom when Lexi stumbled out of the room. "Morning, sleepyhead. It's ten-thirty."

Lexi attempted to say, "Morning," through a yawn.

She stepped into the shower, still half-asleep. As she washed her hair, she wondered about the magic apartment. Her eyes widened.

If the front is in Charlotte and the back is a shack on the edge of a lake, what are the water pipes and electrical cables connected to?

Suspiciously, she peered at the shower and shook her head. "Well, that woke me. It's best not to think about stuff like this."

"Sorry, dear?" Dolores was outside the bathroom.

"Nothing, only…thinking out loud." She scrubbed her face.

Back in the room and dressed, she waited while Scott laced his high-tops and walked to the door.

Lexi cocked an eyebrow. "Where are you going?"

"Dolores has made bacon and pancakes." He turned to her with a grin.

"What about making your bed?"

He frowned. "This room will disappear when we've finished with it."

"That's no excuse. Show some respect."

His shoulders sagged but he rolled his eyes and returned to make the bed. He finished by plumping the pillow. "Happy?"

"Yep." Lexi walked to the door.

Scott looked at her unmade bed. "Hey, how about yours?"

She smirked. "There's no point. This room will disappear when we've finished with it."

"Very funny," he muttered.

With him on her heels, she wandered through to find coffee, piles of bacon, and pancakes waiting for them.

"You won't get it if you don't sit." The vampire held a piece of bacon up and Marcel jumped to try to reach it. "Now sit."

The puppy's butt hit the floor and Dick gave him the bacon. "Good boy."

They ate and prepared to leave. As Lexi stood at the door, she noticed that Dick's bedroom door had disappeared but hers was still there. Curious, she walked down the hallway and glanced at the two beds. Hers was still untidy. She stepped in and made it quickly, then looked around to see if Scott had left his beanie or she'd left a blade somewhere.

Nothing was obvious so she stepped out of the room and walked past the bathroom. She turned to see if she'd left anything in there and grimaced when she faced only a wall. The bedrooms and bathroom were gone.

Dolores stood beside the front door to the little apartment.

"Call me if you need anything." She opened the door and the others filed through. They immediately stood in a cozy diner.

A young woman smiled at them. "Welcome to Southwest Diner."

Lexi glanced over her shoulder. The door to the fae's living room had closed and was now a glass entrance door from the street.

Scott glanced at the specials board on the wall and didn't miss a beat. "Cherry pie, please."

She stared at him in disbelief. "You've just had breakfast."

Dick raised an eyebrow. "He is a growing boy."

The woman laughed. "Let me show you to your table."

They sat at one with a pink check tablecloth next to the window and ordered coffees, one cherry pie, one Bloody Mary, and a bowl of water. Lexi glanced around the room. She noticed a guy who looked like a truck driver staring at the vampire with a perplexed expression from across the room. He saw her looking and returned his gaze to his newspaper.

Scott whirled his finger in a helicopter gesture, which indicated that no one could listen in on their conversation.

"Will your magic work when we get into Vegas?" she asked.

He shrugged. "Probably not all of it. That'll be inconvenient, I guess."

She looked out of the window. "I assume there are no casinos in Boulder, then."

Dick waited for the server to put the drinks down and leave before he spoke. "There are casinos here but they have individual protections on them, the same way many banks and high-end stores do everywhere else. The problem with Vegas is that there are so many casinos, the protection spells clashed. It was a mess. That's why they decided to set up the wards over the whole city." He picked his drink up and looked at it. "It's a mason jar. How quaint." He stirred it with the celery stick, tapped it on the side, and took a large sip.

They talked as they ate and drank, then the vampire pointed when a large white SUV parked outside. "Here's our ride."

Lexi gazed at the shining monster. "Holy smoke! Did Dolores order that?"

"Pfft! Dolores ordered a car. I upgraded it." He leaned forward conspiratorially. "I know for a fact that some of her clients are really rich. I know that because, before I worked for her, I hired her. I don't know why she's so stingy with expenses."

Scott shrugged. "She prefers us to be inconspicuous."

Dick stood and dropped a twenty-dollar tip on the table. "Well, there's being inconspicuous and then there's catching nasty diseases from the motels she puts you in."

The young man narrowed his eyes. "Aren't you staying with us?"

He laughed. "Heavens, no. I have my own place."

Lexi made a mental eye-roll. "Of course you do. Come on, then. Let's go see what palace she's lined up for us today."

CHAPTER THREE

Dick pulled his car into the forecourt of the Vegas motel. Lexi remained silent and studied the building as he parked. They climbed out and the vampire leaned on his car door. "Dear God, it's déjà vu all over again."

Scott squinted with his hand above his eyes. "It looks better than the motel in Palm Springs. This one has a pool."

She looked quickly at Dick. "Oh! You're still here."

He frowned in response. "Sorry?"

"I wondered, with this no magic rule in Vegas, if you'd go whoosh in the sunlight."

His jaw dropped. "Jesus Christ! That didn't even occur to me. Wait, you didn't mention it until now?"

With a shrug, she stepped out and went to pull her small case from the trunk.

The vampire stared open-mouthed from her to Scott, who chuckled.

"She's kidding. Dude, I changed your physiology on a molecular level."

Dick glanced at Lexi as he walked Marcel to a flowerbed filled with weeds to relieve himself. "Are you sure she knows that?"

The sorcerer nodded. "Of course she does. You knew that, didn't you, Lexi? We know that now."

"Hmm?" She looked up as though she hadn't been listening.

Dick raised an eyebrow. "What do you mean by now?"

"I'll be honest. That morning in Cabo after I'd done the spell and the sun was rising, my heart was in my mouth."

"You were one hundred percent certain I was safe. You said so."

"I was—pretty much." Scott pulled his bag onto his shoulder.

Marcel sniffed the weeds, yelped, then ran to the car and peed on a tire.

Dick rolled his eyes and turned to the younger man. "I was about to ask if you'd rather stay in the guest room at my condo."

Lexi took a few steps toward the office, then turned. "No, we'll be fine. We'll see you at the Mob Museum in the morning."

"I wasn't asking, I was rescinding the offer I hadn't made." The vampire stuck his tongue out at her and climbed into the car with Marcel.

The two friends continued to the motel office.

"We're booked in." Lexi took a credit card from her pocket.

"You're in room fifteen. Ground level." The receptionist placed a keycard on the desk.

Scott looked at her, surprised when she took the card. "You never want ground level."

"I don't mind. I'm still tired so I'd sleep right here standing up." She wasn't kidding and wondered when she would get her strength back.

They left the registration office and walked around the pool to room fifteen. She left Scott outside to hold the bags and gaze at the pool while she went in to check the room. The first thing she noticed was the sticky carpet and the Velcro-like sound and resistance when she lifted her feet to step. The walls were dirty, and the bed cover was decidedly threadbare.

She called him in. "It's clean. Well…not clean. I mean it's safe." She added quietly, "On a non-microbial level."

He entered and dropped his bag onto the innermost bed, then approached the bathroom door and pushed it open hesitantly. She retrieved her toiletry bag and shorts from her case when his shoulders relaxed. He stepped out, picked his bag up, and entered the bathroom.

A few minutes later, he emerged with a towel over his shoulder, wearing swimming shorts and a big smile. "I'm going for a quick swim."

"Is your beanie waterproof?" She smirked when he clapped his hand on his head.

"Oh. Ha!" Scott pulled the hat off and threw it on his bed.

When he opened the door, two boys of about ten years old stood at the balconies above, one on either side of the pool, and began a shouted conversation from one side of the motel to the other.

"Hey, Jaden."

"Yeah?"

"It looks like they fished the body out. You wanna go swimming?"

"My mom says I gotta wait until they clean the pool but Mr. Casey says they ain't gonna do that 'til October."

Scott took a hasty step back and flicked the door. It swung shut. He stared at it for a moment before he returned to the bathroom.

When he had dressed and entered the room again, Lexi waited for him with her case in one hand and his beanie in the other. He looked around, confused. "What?"

"This place is a hard no for me. We're not doing it. Let's find somewhere else." She shoved his hat into his hand and marched out of the door and past the other rooms.

He followed hurriedly. "Where will we go, then?"

"We'll get a cab to the Strip. I can't promise the nicest hotel but we'll go somewhere with a halfway decent pool." She rounded the corner to the parking lot and came to a halt so suddenly that he bumped into her.

Dick stood with his sunglasses on, sunning his face as he leaned against the car. Marcel lay in the scant shade at his feet.

Scott backed away and walked around Lexi to the car. "What are you doing here?"

"I'll be honest, it took longer than I expected." The vampire looked at his watch. He opened the passenger door and Marcel jumped in and scrambled into the back of the car. "I contacted a friend who owns the condo next door to mine. We bought them at the same time. It's free for a few days."

They hesitated and Scott said, "Er...we were going—"

Dick put a hand up to stop him. "There are two pools and three hot tubs in the complex."

The young man took several steps forward and wrapped him in a huge hug. "I love you, man." He jumped into the back seat next to Marcel, clicked the seatbelt into place, and grinned.

The vampire looked into the car while he smoothed an eyebrow. "And just like that, the chase is over, the battle won, and the spoils laid at my feet."

Lexi chuckled. "Sorry, Romeo. I think you have a way to go before you can mount that prize...on your wall." She climbed into the car. "So, where are we going?"

He clicked his seatbelt and started the engine. "The complex lies a couple of blocks from the Strip. I've never actually been there."

Scott leaned forward. "I thought you said you owned a condo."

"I do, but I rent it out through an agency. It was a business purchase, but I'm interested to see how they've maintained it."

They arrived at the complex and he ran into the office. When he came out, he dropped a key into Lexi's hand. They walked through the gardens and finally, he pointed as they reached the buildings. "That one's yours." He returned to the car for his case.

Scott stood at the door while she walked around the condo. "What's it like?"

She popped her head around the door. "I feel like I should have taken my boots off. Everything's white."

He followed her through the hallway into the plush living room with its white rugs, white walls, and white furniture. His jaw dropped. "This place is *nice*."

"Good grief!" Dick's voice reverberated through the wall.

Lexi ran out with Scott at her back and they burst into Dick's condo.

She had her katana in hand the moment she was through the door. The vampire stood in the middle of the living room. It wasn't as nice as theirs but nice enough. "What's wrong?" Her gaze darted around in search of potential problems.

His face was a mask of horror. "I paid for top quality furnishings. It looks like Ikea stumbled in drunk and threw up everywhere."

Scott looked around the room. "It looks okay."

The vampire gazed incredulously at the furniture. "Pfft! Okay —okay for you."

Lexi stared at him, amazed that he seemed completely unaware that he was being rude. "Gosh, no. It's not okay for us. Ours is much nicer. Come on, Scott. Let's get those swimming shorts on you." She marched out as she slid her katana into the pocket.

He followed. "All right, but I think I can manage that myself."

Half an hour later, he was in the pool and floated on a giant, triangular, inflatable pizza slice. Lexi lay on a sunbed in her leather pants and linen vest. Dick joined them in his Versace swimming briefs and held a tray of margaritas.

She squinted at him. "It's good to see you've calmed somewhat."

"I've spoken to the management company."

"We heard." She chuckled. "The walls are thin."

"They'll see if they can fix it before I can contact my lawyer on Monday. It's like a race."

"Yes, we heard. Who do you think will win?"

"Them if they have any sense." He handed her a drink and walked to the pool, where Scott sat on the inflatable and paddled to the edge to take a glass. The two men clinked glasses and signaled a toast to Lexi, who reciprocated.

Dick settled himself on the sunbed beside hers. "I've been thinking about this case. Does it ever make you wonder…"

Lexi waited.

He took a sip of his drink before he continued, "Why do they insist on keeping magical objects in museums? This is our second in as many weeks, and that last one certainly wasn't my first."

"Delphine's ring wasn't magical until that boy cast a spell with it."

"Ah, yes. Poor Jamal. But there must be thousands—maybe millions—of objects in museums that belonged to people who don't need to be brought back. All it takes is someone to get hold of Hitler's jockstrap and we're all in trouble."

Lexi coughed as her drink went down the wrong way.

"Are you all right?"

She took another sip. "I'm fine. You're not wrong. That's a thought to give anyone nightmares for all kinds of reasons."

Dick tilted his head, his brow wrinkled. "*Are* you all right? You look tired—weary even."

"The last few days took it out of me," she admitted.

He rolled onto his side to face her. "What was it like wearing the possessed ring?"

"I felt incredibly powerful, but she didn't take over and I didn't feel a compulsion to do her bidding like Lorenzo did. She did talk too much, though. In the few minutes I wore it, she wouldn't shut up. It was so annoying."

He took another sip of his cocktail. "So, snapping Lorenzo's neck like that was all you?"

Lexi recalled how easy it had been to break the vampire's neck with a flick of her wrist. She smirked. "Do you think I should have done it with my thighs?"

"Well, that does seem to be your signature move. It surprised me, though. It all seemed so…casual."

"In my defense, I didn't know it would kill him—like, properly. I guess the zombie bite stopped him from healing. *And* he was about to die anyway. *And* if I hadn't done it that way, I'd probably have done it another way."

"Okay, calm yourself. I'm only saying that the ring must have had some kind of effect. Your eyes went completely black. That didn't happen to Amy, Betsy, or Lorenzo."

Scott walked up to them. "I still need to research the black eyes."

Dick looked at the sorcerer. "Did you see it? I almost ran away after she threw me across the room."

"I didn't mean to do that. I didn't know how strong I was and you were crowding me. I only meant for you to give me some space."

Lexi pulled the stiletto knife from her dimensional pocket and flicked a slice of lime from her drink onto the tray.

The vampire pointed. "Hey, how are you still able to access that pocket? It's magic isn't it?"

Scott sat in a chair next to them. "Some things are acceptable for mages and legacies. Not everything, though. I can't translocate, which is annoying. We can't portal into or out of Vegas and we can't use objects with magical properties. Dolores has had to give us real paperwork for the job. I know it's all so people can't simply stroll in and magic the money out of casinos, but I feel like I have one hand tied behind my back." He looked at Lexi. "Getting back to the black eyes. I'm sure I've read about it happening before. I'll have to look into it." He smiled but it looked forced. "Do you want a top-up?"

She knocked the rest of her cocktail back and held it out to him, and Dick did the same.

He looked at them both. "I meant a magical top-up, but I'll do the drinks too."

Lexi turned her arm to show him. "Look, I'm still full. I'm not leaking unused magic. It must be something to do with the restrictions in place."

Scott smiled. "Cool." He balanced the empty glasses and headed to the bar. She followed him with her gaze. When he was concerned, so was she, and she had felt his concern through their link. She wondered what he wasn't saying.

Dick lay back to enjoy the sun. "Where do you want to eat dinner? Or would you prefer to explore Vegas by yourselves?"

She sighed. "I thought I might turn in early. You two should go out, though, and bring Cheetos. That'll do. She closed her eyes and sighed, soaking in the warmth.

***

"It's up to you. I don't mind." Scott shrugged.

"I don't eat," Dick said for what seemed to be the fiftieth time, "so it's most definitely up to you."

Lexi lifted her sunglasses. "This has been going on for almost an hour. You're like a married couple. Dick, decide where to eat. Take Scott somewhere you think he'd like." She dropped the sunglasses onto her face.

"That works for me." The young man grinned.

"Great. I know a fabulous barbecue place off the Strip. Everyone raves about it, but I think we should go there when we're all out together. Lexi shouldn't miss Jessie Rae's. Scott, I'll take you to The Burger Bar at Mandalay Bay. Everyone I know —well, everyone I know who eats food—tells me they do the best burgers in town and apparently, their shakes are to die for."

She sat quickly. "Thank God that's agreed." She looked at Dick. "How are you doing for rations?"

"I'll eat later. I've ordered in." He didn't offer any further details and she didn't ask.

Instead, she turned to Scott. "Will you get ready?"

"One last swim." He headed to the pool and dropped in.

Dick watched with a somewhat bored expression. "What happened to his floating pizza?"

"The girl it belonged to came and snatched it while you were at the bar."

He raised an eyebrow. "The evil bitch. I hope he turned her into a mung bean."

"She was, like, six."

"And?"

Lexi rolled her eyes. She looked at the pool and smiled. "He's making the most of it. I'm glad we didn't stay at that shitty motel."

Dick stood. "Good for him. I'll start getting ready. I'll meet him out front in forty-five minutes."

Lexi woke in the middle of the night from a vision of flashing lights and the heavy vibration of bass. She lay in the dark and realized it hadn't been a dream. Sometimes, she had a sense of where Scott was when they were apart. It would appear that her two friends were in a club dancing to seventies disco music. She smiled and closed her eyes to sleep again.

A muted thump made her sit. It had come from Dick's condo. She was dressed within sixty seconds, opened the front door silently, and crept out. When she saw no one about, she scurried across to Dick's entrance. She tried it and the door wasn't locked.

With a slow, careful movement, she turned the handle the rest of the way and opened the door silently.

Once again, the katana was in her hand. The house was in darkness, but she could hear someone moving in the living room. Sweat prickled her scalp as she took another silent step forward. The hyperawareness brought a cold sheen along her arms followed by goosebumps. Suddenly her vision blurred, and her stomach lurched. She flailed in the darkness, found the stair rail, and leaned against it.

When she looked up, an eerie glow came from the area ahead. It cast enough light to enable her to see the hallway around her. She rounded the corner into the living room as a large billowing specter came toward her, and she struck out with the katana. A scream pierced the night.

When Lexi turned the light on, Dick's house boy from Palm Springs stood holding half a sheet in each hand. Jesús wore a strange glass pendant, which was the source of the bright yellow glow. Before she could say anything, he looked at her and fainted. She stared across the room and into a mirror on the wall. Her eyes were black.

What's happening to me?

She checked that he hadn't died of fright, then sat on the couch with her face in her hands.

"Lexi?" Jesús half-whispered, his voice trembling.

She raised her head from her hands to where he sat on the floor. He sighed with relief and put a hand on his chest. "I must have been seeing things."

"I'm so sorry." She somehow managed a smile for the shaken young man. "I almost killed you. I thought… I don't know what I thought."

"Mr. Levin asked me to bring some things for him." He held up the ripped sheet and shrugged.

Lexi face-palmed. "Please tell me they're not two-thousand-dollar sheets."

He started to fold them. "No, no, don't worry. They're only the six-hundred-dollar sheets. It's fine. I brought a few."

She couldn't tell if he was joking but suspected not. "Scott and I are staying next door. I heard a noise and came to investigate. What were you doing?"

"Luckily, I had a travel bag in the trunk. I used it to cover the window in the master bedroom, but I had to climb on the dresser to do it." Jesús rubbed his elbow. "I fell off."

"A travel bag?" For the life of her, she couldn't grasp what he meant.

"You know..." He crossed his hands over his chest like a corpse.

"Oh. A body bag. When did you last speak to Mr. Levin?"

"It's been a couple of weeks." The man put his hands on his hips. "Why would he stay here? I looked for a basement, but I couldn't find one so I started on the window. Do you think I did the right thing?"

"I guess you'll have to speak to him about that." She had no idea why Dick hadn't told him about the daywalking, but that was his business.

Jesús gazed around the room. "I thought I was in the wrong place. First the windows, then this furniture. It's horrible."

Lexi wanted to ask him why his pendant was glowing, but she'd had enough. "I'm going back to bed." She turned and left the room.

She wanted to tell Scott about her eyes but what could he do? It seemed he was already nervous about Bryan, which made it unfair to bother him further. She decided to let him enjoy his night out and pretended to be asleep when he came stumbling in at four am.

CHAPTER FOUR

After lying awake for another couple of hours, Lexi got up at six am, made coffee, and sat at a table on the deck outside. She didn't know what to think so she didn't think at all. After an hour of simply blanking out, Dick joined her. "A penny for your thoughts?"

She opened her mouth to make a glib response but nothing emerged.

He tried again. "Well, you scared seven shades of shit out of Jesús last night."

"Sorry about that—and your sheet. I'll ask Scott if he can mend it."

"Don't worry about it." He slid his sunglasses on. "Jesús told me he thought he was hallucinating because your eyes seemed to have turned black."

All she could think to do was shrug because she was at a loss to explain it. She changed the subject. "What time should we head to the Mob Museum?"

The vampire raised an eyebrow at her diversion. "Dolores has arranged for us to meet her friend near the museum for a chat first."

"What the fuck?" Jesús screeched from the doorway. He gazed in horror at his boss, who languished very comfortably in the sunlight without catching fire.

Several people seated outside their apartments eating breakfast stared at him in alarm.

Dick waggled a finger in his ear as though he had deafened him. "Good morning, Jesús. Perhaps you'd like to put some clothes on."

The man leapt back through the door.

Lexi chuckled. "You didn't tell him?"

"I thought I'd surprise him," he said blandly, a small smirk at the corners of his mouth.

"I think that between us, we'll surprise him to death." The smile left her face as she recalled how close she'd been to gutting him. She sighed. "I can't feel Delphine there but what else could it be?"

"Perhaps Scott could…I don't know, have a poke around up there to see if he can find her."

"I don't want to distract him from the job. If we find the guy and get the talisman today, I can talk to him later." She picked her empty mug up and stood.

Dick fixed her with a stern look. "So you're asking me to say nothing to him?"

"I wouldn't ask that of you." She didn't need to and was fairly sure he knew what she expected.

He didn't seem happy about it but nodded and she took that as his agreement. The vampire turned to Jesús, who had put on a pair of shorts and resumed his bemused stare at his boss from the doorway. "We'll head out for the morning. Would you mind looking after Marcel?"

The man nodded. "Yes, Mr. Levin."

They sat at a table in one of the casino restaurants on Fremont and Lexi perused the menu.

Scott slouched like a grumpy teen. "Come on, I'm starving."

She handed the menu to the server. "Eggs over medium with bacon and coffee. Thank you."

The young woman looked at Dick with an expectant smile.

"I'll take a Breakfast Jack." He handed the menu to her without looking at it.

The waitress looked confused. "I'm not sure—"

Scott laughed. "Let me guess. It's a Jack Daniels served at breakfast time."

The vampire nodded and the girl left the table.

Coffee was provided and she listened as the two men chatted and laughed.

Oh, God, they've bonded. Her lip twitched but she said nothing.

Dick took his cell phone out and showed the screen to the other man. They both laughed.

Lexi raised an eyebrow. "If you two are showing each other dick pics, I'll happily move to another table—or restaurant."

"Lexi, please. My good name would never be associated with something so vulgar." He showed her the screen. "We found a restaurant called Chin Chin last night. Peter told me that Chin Chin is Japanese for penis, which is hilarious, so I took a selfie with the restaurant in the background and I'm sending it to him."

She remembered the young blood donor who had almost died after being drugged by Lorenzo in an effort to kill Dick. "How is he?"

The vampire put his cell phone away as the waitress arrived with the food. When she left, he answered, "He says he's taken himself out of the food chain but wants to keep in touch. And he's off the recreational drugs."

"That's probably a good idea. He was lucky he didn't die." Scott splashed ketchup over his impossibly large plate of food and looked at Lexi. "Hey, doesn't this remind you of that break-fast we had in LA that time?"

She stared at the red-covered plate. "No. It reminds me of Jamal's corpse."

"You're trying to put me off my food but it won't happen." He bit defiantly into a piece of bacon.

The two men continued to chat while she ate her breakfast, unable to stop thinking about how close she'd come to hurting Jesús. Scott looked at her occasionally with a concerned expression, which she pretended not to see.

Finally, he finished his food and focused his attention on her. "So, what happened last night? I felt your nerves ramp up. I tried to translocate because I was too drunk to remember I couldn't do that, then I sensed you calm."

Lexi shrugged. "I thought Dick's condo was being robbed. I went in but it was only Jesús, so I went back to bed." She avoided looking at the vampire.

Scott looked guilty. "I'm sorry I wasn't there. If I can't translocate, I shouldn't be so far or let myself get into that state."

She finished her coffee. "It was fine. You do deserve the occasional night off." She wiggled her eyebrows. "Strutting your stuff to 'Dancing Queen' and 'Blame it on the Boogie.'"

"Hey! No spying on the guys' night out." His cheeks went pink.

"A girl can't help what she dreams." She chuckled.

Dick knocked his bourbon back and glanced around the room.

He froze and some of the drink escaped his mouth and splashed onto his shirt. "Dick? Are you okay? You've dribbled half your drink down your shirt."

Dick gasped. "It's fine. The rest of it is in my lungs."

"You must be Dolores' friends. I'm Albin." Lexi looked into the face of a man who was, quite possibly, the most beautiful living being she had ever seen. He was tall and dressed professionally.

His white shirt was stretched tight across his chest and arms, fighting to hold in the muscles beneath it. She put him in the late-thirties. His jaw was chiseled and his chin dimpled, while his eyes were the cornflower-blue that people talked about but, until now, she'd believed didn't exist. His lips turned up playfully at the corners.

Those lips.

She had never seen a specimen like him. Besides, she didn't usually have time for relationships or, God forbid, romance.

But all I want to do right now is grab hold of this man, throw him onto the table and—

"Lexi!" Scott's urgent but quiet warning made her jump. "Can you just…not?" His face was aflame.

"Oops!" She blushed as hotly when she realized that he would have felt her wandering daydream through their link.

"And you are?" Albin directed the full intensity of his heavenly gaze at the vampire.

"Dick," he managed in only a slightly squeakier tone than usual.

"Really? What a coincidence." A slight smile played on Albin's lips. "I've been looking for you." His eyebrow twitched a fraction of an inch and Dick groaned.

Scott turned in his seat to see what was going on. "Oh! Right, I see." He turned, took his cell phone out, placed it on the table, and opened his notes app. "Take a seat. I'm Scott and this is Lexi."

"Hi." The man complied.

Dick stood. "Can I offer you my chair?"

Albin smiled. "I'm fine, thank you. I'm sitting."

"Of course you are, yes." The vampire sat but immediately stood again. "Can I get you something? Coffee? Jewelry?"

"A coffee would be great, thank you."

Dick disappeared.

Albin followed him with his gaze. "He's interesting."

"No, he's not." Lexi couldn't believe she'd blurted that out. From the corner of her eye, she could see Scott staring at her.

The man turned to her. "He's a vampire out at eight am. That's interesting."

She dragged her attention away from the man's face and looked at Dick, who seemed to be fighting the waitress for the coffee jug.

"When did you notice the talisman missing?" Scott tapped his cell.

The vampire returned to the table with a mug and the coffee jug. The bewildered waitress stared at his back, a hundred-dollar bill clutched in her hand.

"Two days ago." Albin leaned back as Dick poured the coffee. His gaze remained glued to the historian's face. "That's enough, thank you."

Dick looked down to see the coffee had poured over the top of the mug. "Good heavens." He snatched the serviettes and mopped the spill.

Scott gave up. He retrieved the coffee jug and refilled his and Lexi's mugs, then waited for the vampire to return to his seat. Finally, he continued. "What do the security cameras show?"

Albin drank carefully from the overfilled mug. "A throng of people—more than usual—around the case. Then the camera went on the fritz. When the crowd cleared, the chip was gone. All the thief left was the little embroidered pouch the talisman had rested on."

Lexi looked at her coffee. It was easier to speak to the Adonis when she wasn't looking at him. "I don't understand why Kindred hasn't taken an interest. It sounds like it was, without doubt, stolen."

"I went to the Strip myself and spoke to the father of the local unit. I had stills from the security camera. Most of it was useless but I think it was clear from the footage before and after that it had been stolen. They looked at me like I was being hysterical."

Dick put his elbow on the table and his chin in his hand. "Those bastards. Would you like me to kill them for you? I could, you know."

"That's very kind of you, but I wouldn't like to start a war because my feelings are hurt."

"How thoughtful," Scott muttered. "Did you have any questions, Lexi?"

"Hmm?"

He put his cell phone away. "No? That's fine. Let's go over there."

Dick bolted out of his seat and held Albin's chair.

Lexi glanced at him and noticed that his fangs were showing. She stared hard at him. "We're out in public. Calm yourself."

The vampire smiled awkwardly. "Oopsie." He followed Albin to the exit.

She turned to face Scott. "What just happened?"

"I have no idea. Let's get out of here." He paid the check.

At the museum, they climbed the steps to the entrance of the building.

"Where are the papers Dolores gave us?" she asked Scott.

He pointed. "Dick has them."

Lexi grimaced when she saw Dick gazing at Albin while the historian removed his ID and lanyard from a pocket. The vampire was fanning himself with the paperwork.

She approached him and took the documents out of his hand "Get a grip."

His expression awed, he gazed at the other man from behind. "But *look* at that."

Unfortunately, she looked and had to agree. He wasn't wrong. Her gaze lingered on Albin's perfect form.

Scott snatched the documents out of her hand. "Get a grip."

The three of them followed their guide into a silent foyer and through another set of doors.

The sorcerer took a map of the exhibit from a display as they moved between the various artifacts.

Albin stopped at a door with a rope across it and a sign that stated the room was closed to the public. He swiped his ID across the pad on the door frame and it let them through. "I can show you what security footage there is," he said and pointed to the cabinet.

Dick tapped him on the shoulder. "I'll come and look at that."

"It's this way." He walked toward a door and the vampire raced ahead and rattled it loudly as he tried to open it for him. The historian held his ID up. "Careful, you'll have that off its hinges."

With an attempt at nonchalance, he smoothed his eyebrow as the other man stepped forward and swiped his ID. "Sorry, I don't know my own strength." He opened the door and followed their guide through.

Lexi stared after them. "Oh, my God. Dick's like a dog in heat."

Scott looked at her with an eyebrow raised and smirked.

"What?" She pointed at the glass display case. "Get on with it, then."

They stared into the cabinet at the label indicating where the lucky poker chip had been displayed before it was stolen.

She looked at him. "Anything?"

He closed his eyes and waved his hands around. "There's no dust and the wards won't let me create an energy ball to follow the magic." He opened his eyes again and looked inside the glass display case. "That might help."

A shiny silver cigarette case lay inside. He opened his hand but nothing happened. "Damn it. I can't get it."

Lexi walked around the case. "I hope Albin's taking care of the security cameras." She dipped to the back of the case and slid her lock-picking tools out. Crouching close to the lock, she set to work. After a minute, she heard the satisfying click. "We're in."

She reached in and snatched the cigarette case as a door opened. In one fluid movement, she had closed the back door of the cabinet and stood next to Scott.

"What are you up to?" A man in a security uniform entered the room.

Scott held the papers out. "We've come to look at this display."

He ignored the documents, took them both by the arm, and led them to the door. "This room is supposed to be closed to the public. Out you get."

"We're not the public. We're here—" Lexi scowled when she realized she was speaking to a closed door and knocked peremptorily.

Scott looked at the security scanner beside it. "Is there any way you can break into this?"

Lexi glanced at it. "I could shoot it." She hammered on the door again with her fist.

"Would that open the door?"

"Probably not." She grasped the handle and rattled the door. "Open, you son of—" She felt a jolt of magical energy and the door opened.

The sorcerer looked at it. "That shouldn't have worked." He created a ball of energy in his palm. "The wards are down." He extinguished the orb and they raced into the room. There was no sign of the security man. They ran to the door Dick and Albin had used and along a hallway, looking into each room as they passed. Finally, they entered the security office.

It took a moment for Lexi to interpret what she saw. Albin stood with a hand over his neck and Dick was at the other end of the room with his shirt off and his fangs protruding.

"I'm so sorry. I don't know what came over me." The vampire looked horrified. His face was scarlet as he scrambled to replace his shirt.

"It's okay, honestly. It happens more often than you'd think." The historian removed his hand to reveal a scratch.

Dick pushed past Lexi and Scott and out of the office.

She stared at the screens, then turned to the other man. "I assume you didn't see what happened out there."

He sighed. "The wards went down again?" With a scowl, he went to a screen and rewound the footage. "It's the same as last time. Here you are, looking into the case. It goes blank, then the picture comes back—" Albin looked closely at the screen, then bolted from the room. They ran after him and the three of them gathered around the display case.

Albin tapped the glass. "Did you take anything out of here?"

Lexi showed him the cigarette case. "Yes, this. Scott can use it to help in the investigation."

"Of course, for the reflection." He nodded. "Good thinking. And the pouch?"

She looked into the display. The little embroidered pouch was also missing. "Could I have knocked it down?"

The historian retrieved a key and opened the back of the cabinet. He searched quickly but carefully for the missing item. "It's definitely gone. What happened?"

His frown deepened when she told him about the security man throwing them out of the room.

He shook his head. "Why would someone go to such lengths to take the pouch? It makes no sense."

Dick rejoined them. His shirt was on but his face was still pink and he didn't seem to be in a hurry to make eye-contact with anyone.

Lexi looked at him. "I didn't know vampires could blush."

Albin's lips twitched. "Blushing is simply what happens when all the blood rushes to one place in the body in response to emotional or physical stimuli."

The man waited for Dick to look at him, then winked at the blushing vampire. He turned to Scott. "Will your reflection spell work within the wards?"

Scott looked doubtful. "Probably not but we can try."

Lexi turned in surprise. "Why not? It seems like an innocent enough spell."

"Until you use it to spy on someone entering a safe combination." The sorcerer shrugged.

She raised an eyebrow. "Okay, I never thought of that."

They headed to the employee section and into Albin's office.

Scott took the cigarette case out. "If it works, it would be better with a mirror."

Her quick scan around the office didn't reveal one, but the historian took a lab coat off a hook on the wall to reveal a mirror beneath it. She looked at him, her expression curious.

"I hate mirrors," he explained simply.

Lexi shook her head. *If I looked like him, I'd walk around naked in a hall of mirrors all day long.*

Scott held the case up to it and muttered a few words but nothing happened. "Nope, it's not working."

"It was a long shot. I have to go and wipe you from the security cameras before the day shift starts." Their guide led them to the exit. "Perhaps we could meet later?"

The sorcerer nodded. "Beyond the wards? Then you can see the reflection yourself."

Albin handed Lexi a card with his address on it. "I don't go beyond the wards. You look at it and let me know. I'll see you at eight." He turned to Dick and handed him a card. "And I'll see *you* at six."

Scott looked at the card over Lexi's shoulder. "Park Towers—sounds nice."

The historian shrugged. "It's a roof over my head."

They said goodbye and returned to the car.

Lexi opened the passenger door. "How far out do the wards stop working?"

Dick climbed into the driver's seat. "I have no idea, but I don't want to stop every mile to check. Let's head to Boulder. Southwest Diner?"

Scott's head popped into the space between the seats. "Sure. It's almost an hour since I last ate."

After they had been driving for a couple of minutes, Lexi turned to the vampire. "What happened to you back there?"

He gave her a wide and slightly hysterical-looking grin. "Let's put music on, shall we?"

When they pulled up at the diner, they didn't leave the car.

Lexi looked into the eyes of the truck driver, who was seated at the same table as before. "Doesn't that guy have a home to go to?"

Scott looked out. "Who?"

She was about to point him out but he was no longer staring at them. "Never mind."

The sorcerer shuffled across the back seat and settled himself in the middle. He held the cigarette case up facing the rearview mirror and muttered his quiet words.

First, they could see little of interest. He rolled back and it showed them looking at the case before they left the museum. From there, he whirled back what the shiny case had reflected for the previous couple of days. Finally, he stopped it and allowed it to play forward. They watched as a man approached the cabinet.

Lexi pointed. "That's the douche who kicked us out."

The man gazed at the display for a few moments before he walked out of sight. A minute later, a hand appeared from the rear of the cabinet and picked up a golden poker chip. The stranger walked quickly out of view.

Dick pinched his bottom lip as he thought. "Can you put it back to the start and record it on a cell phone?"

Scott reversed the playback in the mirror and passed his cell phone to the vampire, who videoed the theft, then took close-ups of the security guard's face.

When he clicked the cell phone off, he turned to Lexi. "We don't need to bother going into the diner then."

The young man slumped in the seat. "I wanted to try the apple pie this time."

"What are you, twelve?" Dick looked at him in the rearview mirror. "Get a slice to take out, then."

Scott grinned and jumped out of the car.

Lexi opened the passenger door and shouted, "Scott...get two." She smirked at Dick. "I understand why you'd want to get back. You only have eight hours to prepare for your date."

He smoothed an eyebrow in his habitual tell. "Oh, I don't know that I'd call it a date." He giggled. "It's totally a date, though, right? And you're quite correct, looking this good doesn't happen by itself." He sighed. "This must be what it's like to go on a date with me. How thrilling."

She shook her head and chuckled.

CHAPTER FIVE

Scott gazed sadly at his empty plate. "That was the best pie I've ever eaten. What's next?"

Lexi stood and dropped the empty boxes in the trash. "It seems like a waste of time to spend the whole day doing nothing. We should have gone straight to the museum to show Albin the picture. Did you get the impression he wanted us out of the way?"

"It was probably because of what happened with Dick," he shrugged. "We could spend the day by the pool."

She looked at the time. "Scott, do me a favor. Step outside for a moment, please."

He narrowed his eyes. "Okay…" He stepped out onto the deck. "Holy shit. How hot is that?"

"It's August in Las Vegas. I'm not sitting outside in the middle of the day."

"It wasn't this hot yesterday." He sounded sulky.

"It was almost sundown when we went to the pool yesterday."

Scott gazed mournfully at the water. "I wonder if I could run really fast and jump in. I miss translocation. I miss it so much." He closed the door and walked into the kitchen. "What's on tv?"

"I don't know." Lexi narrowed her eyes at him. "Not Star Wars."

"Barbarian!"

The door burst open and Dick flew in. "Jesus, it's hotter than hell out there."

The young man stared at him. "Are you wearing a t-shirt? Like regular people?"

"That's why I'm here. I have nothing to wear. We have to go to the Strip."

Lexi narrowed her eyes. "And *we* need to go with you because?"

"You're my compadres. I need help."

She raised an eyebrow. "You need someone to stand around and tell you you're stunning."

"That's what I said. I need help."

"Fine." She rolled her eyes. "We were only going to watch tv anyway."

Dick grinned. "I know. The walls are terribly thin."

Ten minutes later, they headed to the car. The vampire shouted instructions to Jesús. "Don't let Marcel outside. My poor baby will fry in this heat."

Once they'd left the car with valet parking, they entered the Crystals shopping mall. Lexi consulted the store map and started walking.

"Where are you going?" Dick called after her.

"Versace is this way." She pointed.

"I might not want to buy from Versace. Let's go up to Gucci." He marched ahead and they followed.

Where she stood behind him on the escalator, Lexi whispered to Scott. "He'll drag us around this whole place and I can guarantee you, he'll end up buying from Versace."

Dick didn't turn and merely called in a sing-song voice, "I can hear you."

"I know," she responded in the same tone.

Four hours later, Lexi and Scott waited for him to pay for his purchases in Versace.

He glanced at Lexi while he waited for the tags to be cut off. "Don't look at me like that. I can't simply buy the first thing I see. I need to be sure."

She smiled and was about to respond with "I told you so," when her cell rang. She looked at the display, then answered. "Hi, Dolores."

"Are you hard at work?"

"We're hard at work helping Dick choose a shirt for his date tonight."

"Well, now you're back to work. Someone has stolen a bag of money from a casino. I suspect it might be related to the talisman."

Lexi walked to a quiet corner to hear her better. "Why do you think that?"

"A security guard transporting money from the Bellagio to an armored vehicle tripped and dropped a bag of cash. A man approached, picked the bag up, and walked away with it. Two guards gave chase and somehow ran into each other and knocked themselves out, and a third tried to shoot the thief. His gun fell to pieces in his hand."

She frowned. "Wow! That was all very…unlucky."

"Or lucky, depending on whose perspective you're looking at it from. The bag has a tracker inside it and has been traced to one of the MGM Signature buildings. Be careful. Kindred has been alerted and they'll probably be in attendance."

"Okay, we're on it." She disconnected and hurried to Scott. "Where's Dick?" she asked and looked around.

"He's gone to change into his new clothes. He's due at Albin's in half an hour."

Lexi repeated what Dolores had told her. "We need to hustle. Let him know what's happening and tell him we'll see him at Albin's at eight."

He walked to the changing rooms and was back in seconds. "He'll come if we need him. I said we'd call. He says the hotel is across the street." As they walked, he retrieved his cell, opened the maps app, and directed them to the closest exit.

She turned to him as they approached the MGM Signature buildings. "We're right across the street from that mall. How did it take us a full half-hour to get here?"

"In retrospect, it would have been better to get Dick to drop us off." Scott looked at his watch. "He'll be at Albin's by now. I hope the new clothes have impressed him because my feet are killing me."

Lexi looked across the street at the building's security office. "How can we get past them with no magic?"

Scott pulled their documents out. "This should help."

They crossed the street and approached the security guard. She opened her mouth to speak when an ambulance screeched to a halt and turned in. The security guard ran to release the vehicle barrier. They took advantage of the distraction and walked through.

He gazed at the three golden high-rise buildings. "Do we know which one it is?"

She walked faster. "I have a bad feeling. I think we should follow the ambulance."

The commotion drew them to the correct building. They rounded the corner as the ambulance crew moved to cover a body that had clearly fallen from very high up.

Scott leaned close to her ear. "Was that our guy?"

Lexi stared at him. "Can you imagine how far he fell? I couldn't even tell if that was human."

A group of men leaving the building caught her attention. She grabbed her friend and pulled him around the corner. "I think that's the mage who performs on the Strip."

He snuck his head out and withdrew it quickly. "I've definitely seen him on billboards and tv."

They wandered to the back of a crowd of onlookers. Hidden behind them, they were able to amble around the corner to listen more closely to the men and what appeared to be the end of the conversation.

Someone—presumably the mage—asked, "Are you sure there was absolutely nothing on the body? Nothing in his pockets?"

"Like what?" another man asked.

The first voice answered impatiently. "A golden casino chip."

"No, nothing. That's strangely specific."

The mage sighed. "Forget I said anything about the chip."

"Like what?" The man repeated his question and sounded a little confused.

"Oh, I don't know. I thought maybe the tracker had stopped working because it shattered on impact."

"Oh, I see. That's good thinking, but no. There wasn't a cent in his pocket." The voices grew quieter, so Lexi and Scott moved behind the crowd again.

When the people saw the mage, they recognized him as the famous magician and turned their cameras from the corpse to him.

Unaffected by the attention, he continued. "If the security tracker in the bag was here one minute and gone the next, he must have deactivated it and stashed the bag before he threw himself off the balcony. Search for the bag. I'm on stage in an hour. If you haven't found it tonight, I'll see what I can do, but I can assure you that the wards are still in place."

Lexi was suddenly aware that the crowd around them had begun to disperse. She and her companion looked at each other, certain they were about to be revealed.

Scott said, "Eww—is that his guts in the grass over there?"

The crowd turned and huddled to stare in the direction of the covered corpse again. When the mage had moved out of sight, the two left the way they had entered.

Back on the Strip, Lexi called Dolores to tell her the thief was dead. She explained that the wards had stopped working at least twice that day.

"It sounds like Kindred knows the talisman has been stolen." She stood in the shade with the cell phone on speaker. "The mage asked about it and counseled someone in front of a crowd of people. Why do you think they've denied it's been stolen?"

Her boss was silent for a few moments. "Probably because it calls the wards into question."

After a little thought, she decided it made sense. "About the wards—who could bring them down?"

Dolores paused for a moment. "No single group can do it. It would require the Kindred council and the Fae Council of Elders."

Lexi looked at Scott as he released a frustrated breath. She knew he had the same thought as her—some kind of alliance between Caleb and the Elders. She turned to the cell. "We're going to see Albin in an hour to see if he recognizes the guard. I guess we should have returned to the museum earlier."

The fae tutted. "Oh, dear. You'll be lucky to find him. I expect Albin has sequestered himself somewhere."

The young people shared a puzzled expression. She asked, "Why would he do that?"

Dolores' voice sounded hesitant through the speaker. "He wouldn't want to be caught with someone while the wards are down." She waited for her boss to continue. "You did realize he's an incubus, didn't you? Good heavens, I hope he's alone. I pity anyone who's with him when the wards are down."

"I'll call you later." Lexi disconnected the call. She closed her eyes and sighed. "Of course. That explains it."

They hurried to a line of cabs. "I've heard of incubi," Scott muttered, "but I'm not certain what they do."

"It's a demon. They are irresistible and use that ability to gain control over their victims to plant their demonic seed." She clenched her fist. "Dammit! I knew he was too good to be true. We need to get there. Dick could be in real danger."

They reached the opulent high-rise apartment block twenty minutes later. The sorcerer stared at his phone. "I've tried Dick about fifty times. There's still no answer."

The elevator opened onto the floor and they found the right door. "It's almost seven. He's been in there an hour."

Lexi drew her katana. She raised her hand to knock on the door but Scott stopped her.

"Wait." He held his hand out, palm up.

"What are you doing?"

"I tried to do some magic I know would be restricted. We have no other way to know whether the wards are up or down right now. It looks like they're up."

She nodded, then knocked.

A few moments later, Albin opened the door wearing nothing but a towel around his hips. "You're early."

Lexi paused and stared at his sculpted face and muscled arms. Her gaze traced the muscles from his chest to his towel "Wow!" Her eyeballs sent signals to parts of her body she didn't need to think about in that moment.

"Lexi… Lexi," Scott muttered urgently. She slid her gaze to him. "Breathe."

With an impatient shake of her head, she pushed Albin back into the room. "What have you done with Dick?"

"Do you want to know everything?" His lip twitched. "Well, let me think."

"Is everything okay?" the vampire called from another room.

"It's Lexi and Scott. I think they've come to warn you I'm an incubus."

Dick walked into the room with wet hair, wearing a hotel robe and with a cut crystal glass in his hand. He looked at Lexi. "Oh, I know that, silly." He took a sip of the drink. "Did you find the talisman?"

She shook her head. "It appears the thief threw himself from the balcony of the hotel."

He raised an eyebrow. "Appears? Do you think he might have had a little help?"

"I'd bet money on it." She folded her arms.

The historian gestured expansively. "Well, you're in the right town."

Scott turned to Dick. "Were you here on time?"

Albin snorted.

The vampire looked offended. "I would have been on time, but I stumbled into Tiffany on my way to the car."

Lexi looked at their host. "Where were you this afternoon?"

He walked to the bar and held his hand out for Dick's glass. "I was concerned about the wards so I came straight home to be alone. I almost canceled our meetings this evening."

She nodded. "It's a good thing you came home. The wards have definitely come down twice today. Once to steal the pouch and once to steal the money from the casino. I suspect it might have happened again at around six pm."

Scott turned to her, surprised. "When the guy went off the balcony?"

"It sounds like the money's gone." She nodded. "It would only take a few seconds for a mage to translocate in, throw the guy off the balcony, and disappear with the cash."

Dick raised his hand "Excuse me, but doesn't that constitute the exact opposite of lucky?"

Albin released a relieved breath. "Thank goodness I was alone and you were late."

"Dick was saved by his tardiness." Lexi pulled out the silver cigarette case and handed it to the man.

The vampire chuckled. "I wasn't tardy, I was fashionably late. Anyway, I'm not the one who would have been in trouble. Albin would have been incredibly irresistible. I would have become…bitey."

"Oh. Sorry." She was embarrassed that she'd made sweeping assumptions.

He shrugged and patted her on the shoulder. "Don't worry, I'm quite flattered that you came to save me. I'll get dressed and you can show Albin the video."

The historian looked at his towel and blushed. "Yes, of course. Help yourselves to drinks. I'll make myself more presentable."

Lexi watched him disappear through the door and felt a little disappointed that he would get dressed.

The moment he closed the door, Scott turned to her. "It's a roof over his head."

She studied the huge apartment with its high ceilings, curved windows, grand piano, and lavish furnishings. "I bet Dick's in heaven with this furniture."

"And you'd win that bet," the vampire called.

Albin returned in jeans and a polo shirt. She looked at him and sighed.

"How do incubi get on if they don't live in a warded city?" the sorcerer asked. "It can't be very practical walking down the street and having humans diving onto them in a frenzy."

"We're supposed to be able to turn it on and off. I was cursed, so I have to stay within wards, be protected by some other magic means, or put a bag over my head."

Scott took the cell phone from his pocket. "Who cursed you?"

"My father. He cursed me and disowned me."

Lexi sighed. "I thought our families were bad."

"The whole point of an incubus is to impregnate women. That was supposed to be my job."

The young man scrolled through the cell phone and glanced at him. "You didn't want to do that?"

"It may have escaped your notice, but I don't like girls in that way."

Dammit!

"Praise the Lord," Dick responded from the bedroom.

Scott shook his head and started the video. Lexi pointed to the screen. "That's the guy who threw us out of the room at the museum."

He watched as the thief walked out of sight. The hand came through from the back of the case and grasped the gold poker chip.

When the video ended, he gave Scott his email address and he sent the video file to him.

That done, the sorcerer put his cell into his pocket. "There you go. The guard did it."

Albin raised an eyebrow. "Except that I've never seen that guy before. He didn't work at the museum."

Scott looked crestfallen.

Dick entered the room wearing his new black shirt with the Barocco printed collar. "Was the jumper definitely the guy from the museum?"

Lexi wiggled her head from side to side noncommittally. "Honestly? It's difficult to say. His head looked like spaghetti and meatballs."

The vampire rolled his eyes. "Charming."

CHAPTER SIX

Lexi woke to the sound of her cell phone ringing. She answered it with her usual early-morning disapproval. "Urgh! Oh! Hi, Dolores. Another one?" She continued to listen as she sat and yanked one of the rolled socks out of her boot and threw it at Scott's head. "Wake up." It hit his face and landed next to his nose.

"Gross." He threw the sock at her and they both stared as it burst into flames mid-flight. She batted it away. His eyes went wild as he leapt to pick her boot up and pounded it until the flames were out.

She returned to the phone. "Let me guess, the wards are down again." Lexi walked into the bathroom still with the phone at her ear.

Scott thumped the wall between their and Dick's condo and shouted, "We're up."

"I know. Dolores called me first." The vampire stood in the doorway with two cups of coffee. "I was able to warn Albin about the wards." He passed a cup to Scott.

"Did you reach him in time?" Lexi called from the bathroom.

"Barely. He was heading to the door but he's called in sick."

Dick took a sip of coffee absent-mindedly and spluttered. He stared at the cup in his hand as though it were an alien, then began to heave.

Lexi walked into the room and took it from him. "Thanks." She watched him retch and slapped him on the back. "Are you okay?"

He pointed at the mug in her hand.

"It amazes me that you vamps can tolerate alcohol at all. I think coffee might be a step too far." She took a gulp and rummaged through her dimensional pocket for another pair of socks.

Dick recovered and shook his head. "With alcohol, the higher proof, the better. The margaritas are pure, dogged determination. I don't know what I was thinking, drinking coffee. Perhaps the daywalking has gone to my head. I'll order McRibs next. Then I'll know I'm ready for the final death."

Scott looked up. "I love McRibs."

The vampire shuddered.

Scott looked from one to the other. "So, what's happened? Why are the wards down?"

She put her hand into her dimensional pocket and thought, *clean panties*. When she pulled a pair from her pocket, she gave them a sniff. *Just to be sure.*

"Dear God." Dick turned away from her to Scott. "I'll tell you outside."

As the two men exited, he began the story she'd been told by Dolores. "Someone had a very lucky win at one of the casinos last night."

They stood at the security desk in New York, New York while Lexi showed the Security officer the forms Dolores had given them. "We merely need to look at the video feed of your lucky customer from last night."

The man gazed at the papers, nodded, and turned away to speak into his radio.

Dick leaned forward and tried to read the documents. "What does it say?" he whispered.

Scott shrugged. "I don't know. I haven't read it. Lexi?"

She responded with a mirrored shrug.

The vampire rolled his eyes. "The lack of professionalism in this team disturbs me. We'll probably get arrested."

The man turned to them. "This way."

Dick appeared disappointed that they hadn't been challenged.

They followed their guide to a control room with banks of screens and people watching them. He led them to a workstation at the back of the room where a young Asian man sat in front of several screens.

The security officer tapped him on the shoulder. "Okay, Mo, go ahead."

They watched the recording in silence. Mo pressed pause, then zoomed in on the man's face. "This is him. He's not in our database." He pressed play again.

No one spoke as the feed showed an average man in his fifties—wearing a Hawaiian shirt and carrying a large cocktail—won on the roulette table a few times in succession. He moved to the craps table and repeated the process. A large crowd gathered around him.

After a few minutes, Lexi asked, "How long does this go on for?"

Mo paused it and spun in his chair. "About an hour and a half. He cashed out at one-point-four million."

Dick whistled. "So who is he?"

The man checked his paperwork. "Melvyn Dunk from Idaho."

She frowned at the paused screen. "Any idea where he might be now?"

He looked at his notes, which was a list headed *Time and Activity*. "Still in his suite."

Scott looked openly surprised. "He's here?"

"Of course. We comped him a suite and we're taking his 'wife' shopping today." He very deliberately added air-quotes around the word "wife."

Dick nodded. "While he'll be in the casino giving you the chance to win your money back."

"That's what it's all about." Mo spun to face the screen. "But we can't work out how he did it."

The sorcerer frowned. "There's no chance he won fairly? Surely it must be statistically possible."

In response, the security officer chuckled. "Melvyn left the world of believable statistics a long time before his run ended. He also shot straight through the land of outlandish possibilities and out the other side of dumb luck. Nope. Melvyn cheated and finding out how is more important to us than getting the money back."

"Leave that to us," Lexi answered. "Are you sure he's still in his suite?"

"Yes. The wife left half an hour ago for her free treatments in our spa. I mean, the 'wife.'" He did the air quotes again with a smirk on his face.

"Yes, I get it. He's with a hooker." She made a mental eye-roll. "Which room?"

Mo looked at a screen and read a suite number out. She noticed that conveniently, one of the security cameras was in the hallway directly outside that room.

She smiled. "I'd like to meet Mr. Dunk. Give me a bunch of flowers and a bottle of champagne."

The security guy's eyes traveled down her body and seemed to take in the leather jacket and tight leather pants. "You don't exactly look like a representative of this hotel." He studied the three of them. "In fact, he's the only one who does."

Dick's face lit up. "Why, thank you."

Lexi stared at the man and continued to do so when she didn't receive the response she expected.

"Right, well…I'll get that sorted for you." He swallowed a little nervously and turned to his radio.

Once he nodded confirmation that arrangements had been made, the team headed to the elevators where a young man waited with the champagne and flowers.

She entered the elevator while Scott took the flowers. Dick held the champagne and sneered when he looked at the label. The hotel employee entered the elevator behind them, and they continued to the room in silence.

When Lexi knocked on the door, there was no answer.

"Mr. Dunk?" She knocked again as she called through the door. "I have gifts from the hotel management."

Once again, no answer was forthcoming.

After a few moments, she stepped aside and gestured to their escort to use the keycard. He opened the door and stood in the doorway. A little of the room was visible behind the security officer—a huge spa bath along the left wall. She had to peek around the man to see why he appeared to have frozen on the spot. Melvyn Dunk lay on the bed at the far end of the room with his throat cut.

"Mr. Dunk appears to have run out of luck," Dick muttered.

Lexi put her hand into her pocket to retrieve a weapon.

"Security cameras," the vampire reminded her softly.

The young man uttered a strangled cry, shook himself, and bolted out and down the hallway. She stepped out after him, turned to face the camera and looked into it. "We need to see the"—she held her fingers in little air quotes—"wife."

She lowered her hands and returned to the room, which was partially sectioned off midway down on the right by what looked like a large, floor-to-ceiling closet. It gave the large space the feel of a suite of rooms and partially blocked the view of half the room. A case lay on the bed and she suspected it either held or had held the money. She wanted a peek.

Lexi turned toward the unexplored section and gestured for the men to keep an eye on the grisly scene. "Stay here." She stepped into the room and was only a few steps in, having reached the spa bath, when a man darted from the hidden side of the room. It was the security guard from the museum, now in jeans and a baseball cap. As he snatched the case, he noticed her, shock on his face. He bolted behind the closet and out of view.

With a yell, she broke into a run, raced after him around the corner of the cupboard, and expected to see he had entered from a connecting room. Before she could stop herself, though, she raced through a fae door.

Shocked, she stopped and realized she was in a forest not at all like the one surrounding the glade Scott had described to her. This one smelled unhealthy, stagnant, and decaying. The man sprinted through the woods in front of her. She spun but the fae door was gone.

"Oh, shit."

With no way to go back, she gave chase. She tried to tie his laces, but it didn't slow him. It occurred to her that he probably didn't wear any. She gained ground slowly and thought about the energy ball Scott had created. It was time for a little on-the-job learning. She touched the scar.

I'll have one of those energy balls, please.

The ball appeared on cue but didn't grow in her hand the way her friend's had. It was simply there and about the size of a basketball. She wished she'd taken the time to let Scott teach her how to create them properly because this seemed large. Unfortunately, she didn't know what size it should be for this purpose, nor was she sure how best to throw it.

How hard can it be? I'm a perfect shot with a blade.

She simply lobbed it as best she could. As she did so, a root seemed to rise and trip her and she tumbled awkwardly. She scrambled to her feet as the ball hit a tree.

The trunk exploded

Oops!

Lexi landed hard again and the man was thrown sideways. His hat came off and she could make out pointed ears. It wasn't a surprise.

Quickly, she conjured another ball but visualized one half the size. The ball appeared and seemed better proportioned than her previous one. She hurled it as he created another fae door and disappeared. Her projectile flew past the portal and damaged another tree.

"Oh no, you don't." She increased her speed. When she was almost at the door, something on the ground drew her attention and she immediately recognized the little silk pouch. She stooped, scooped it up, and launched herself through the portal before it could close.

A loud crack heralded her impact with hard concrete. She swore and hugged her arm, sure from the immense pain that she'd broken it. It was a shock because she'd never broken a bone in her life. An extra-strong bone structure was one of the benefits of being a legacy that she did enjoy.

She didn't recognize the building she was in but a quick scan revealed it to be the entrance of a parking garage. In search of her quarry, she ran out to the street and searched the throngs of people who bustled past. Her hasty scrutiny revealed nothing, though, and she glanced into the garage in bewilderment. He stood a few feet from where she'd landed.

The fae door she'd arrived through had vanished and another lay behind it. The criminal lurked on the other side of it, stared directly at her, and grinned.

"You sneaky fucker." She tried to make another energy ball, but she was out of magic. His grin widened before he disappeared.

Lexi stumbled into the street, hugged her arm across her chest, and joined the crowds.

When she reached the intersection, she looked around in bemusement. "Holy shit, I'm in Times Square."

A woman glanced disapprovingly in her direction but not directly at her, then strode on.

Completely disoriented, she leaned against a wall. Her arm throbbed from the pain and she felt queasy. She reached for her dimensional pocket, but her fingertips met her leather pants. Bewildered, she tried a few times with the same result.

What the fuck?

She looked at her scar and gasped when she saw it was gone. All that was visible was the fine silver line that ran along the inside of her arm, which was how people with no magic saw the unhealing scar. Her heart began to race. "Where's my magic?"

"Honey, all the magic's gone from this world. Sadness is all there is."

Lexi looked at a homeless woman bundled in blankets in the doorway beside her. She made another attempt to access her pocket with her good arm, with the same result.

The impossibilities crowded in and she couldn't think. "I need to get off the street."

"So do I, baby, so do I."

She stumbled past the woman, along the street, and into a coffee shop.

The barista stared at her as she staggered in as though he expected her to be trouble. She wondered if he thought she was drunk or on drugs.

Distracted by everything and a little panicked, she spoke to the barista while she scanned for an empty table. "I…was mugged. I need to call my mage."

"Your what?"

Lexi grimaced and turned to him. "My…friend."

He sneered at her. "You have to buy something if you want to sit."

"Jesus, man." A guy spoke from a table near the counter. She turned to see he was seated with a young woman. They both looked at her with concern. "She's been mugged, it looks like she's hurt, and you want to throw her out? I'll buy her a coffee, okay?"

She was embarrassed but fortunately, remembered her emergency cash. "Wait, I have money, thanks. I have money."

Quickly, she turned to the barista and slipped two fingers into her vest. His eyebrows raised but she noticed that he didn't look away. "A triple-shot extra-large latte."

It was awkward because the little seam in the vest where she kept a rolled-up twenty-dollar note was more naturally approached with the other hand. Still, she managed to access it and dropped it onto the counter.

He looked at it and rolled his eyes as he flattened it. Seriously, he had begun to get on her nerves. He rang up the sale and gave her the change. "What name?"

She smirked, then grimaced as her arm jostled a little. "I'll spell it. E-Y-M-A-D." She paused. "I-C".

The idiot frowned but wrote on the cup. "That's unusual."

"It's Dutch." She nodded to the couple and moved to a table in the corner next to the window.

Lexi looked at the pouch. It was empty. She stuffed it into a back pocket and tried to make sense of what had happened.

I can't see my scar. I have to assume I've used all Scott's magic. Maybe I've never exhausted this much magic before. It could have been the energy balls.

She closed her eyes and reached out for her friend but they snapped open when she couldn't feel him. Now, she began to truly panic and wondered what had happened to him.

Were there more fae but I didn't see them? Is he dead?

She couldn't ever not feel him. He was always there and with his absence came real fear.

"I'm a dick. I'm a dick," shouted the Barista.

"I know you are, but what am I?" The young man and his companion both laughed.

"I'm—" the Barista closed his mouth and looked at the name he was reading out. He glared at Lexi, put the cup on the end of the counter, and walked away to serve a young couple who had walked in.

With a smirk, she collected it and decided she felt a little better. After levering the lid off with her teeth and pouring a mountain of sugar into her latte, she returned to the table and her thoughts. She'd have to call Scott.

"Damn it. My phone's in that goddamn pocket."

A man working on his laptop glanced at her. She returned to her thoughts.

The couple at the counter walked to the table next to hers and sat. She looked at them and met the eyes of the young woman, who was thin and pale and looked like a timid, quivering mouse. Lexi glanced quickly at the young man. He didn't seem to look at her but she felt somehow that he was very aware of her. She knew she must look a sight. Her arm was swelling and wasn't the color it usually was.

She wondered if she could find a pay phone or borrow a cell to call Dolores. That immediately raised the next problem and she facepalmed. *I don't know anyone's number. God, could this get any worse?*

To calm herself, she drank more coffee, closed her eyes, and took stock of her situation. *No money, no cell phone, and barely any weapons.* She rocked her head to the left, then the right, and cracked her neck.

Lexi's eyes snapped open. *If I'm no longer connected to Scott or have access to his magic, do I still have his shield? Or can I now be traced by Kindred?*

She glanced at the girl again and their eyes met.

She's Kindred. The idea seemed to come from nowhere, but she knew it to the very core of her. Not only that, she had a good idea who the girl and her partner might be.

Her senses picked up a thrumming excitement in the young man's body—the telltale sign of anticipation.

He's here to kill me, but I'm not in any condition to fight. She sighed. *There's one number I know by heart.*

Lexi stood, picked her coffee up, and made her way to the couple seated near the counter. She pulled a chair closer with her good arm and sat. "I'm sorry to bother you. I wonder if I could borrow your cell to make a call to my…family?"

If they even remember me. It hadn't even occurred to her until that moment that her family could have been counseled. She might have been erased from their minds in the same way Bryan had been erased from hers.

"Of course." The guy put his password in and passed it to her.

She typed the number in, held the cell phone to her ear, and waited for a few seconds.

"Hello?" Hearing the woman's voice almost made her cry. "Hi, Maggie. Remember me?"

"Lexi? Oh, my God. Lexi? Are you okay? Where are you?" Maggie *was* crying.

Lexi swallowed. "Can you come and get me?"

"We haven't been able to find you. Where are you?"

"You'll be able to find me now." Lexi closed her eyes. She disconnected and handed the cell to the young man. "Thank you."

"Do you need money?" the woman asked.

"No, I don't. They're not far. They'll be here soon."

The buzzer on the door sounded and Lexi looked in as a man entered and made eye contact with the Kindred couple. One of his eyes was white. *Eric.* Another man entered behind him and remained at the door.

She hoped her old unit would arrive in time to help her. Then again, maybe they would help their fellow Kindreds instead.

"Thanks for your help. You've been really kind." She glanced around the room and wondered how many patrons might be injured in the fight that was about to break out. That made it an easy decision to take it away from the couple who had helped her.

Lexi stood and headed to the ladies' bathroom. Cradling her arm, she turned and bumped the door open with her butt. Inside, she glanced in a mirror and grimaced. She'd never seen herself so pale. Wearily, she walked to the end of the stalls and entered the last one, closed the door behind her, and locked it.

In the few minutes she had, she took stock. She was down to what was in her vest and pants and what she could use. The garotte was out as she didn't have the mobility to use it. She had two shurikens on her vest, one outside and one inside, and various little blades hidden in seams.

The outer door to the bathroom opened and someone walked in. Her senses told her it was the Kindred girl.

Casually, she unlocked the stall door and stepped out. She looked at the gaunt figure. "I'm sorry. Dolores told me your name but I can't remember it."

"Lucy."

"That's right, and Warren?" she asked.

Lucy nodded.

Lexi remembered her boss appearing from her dimensional pocket after being attacked by Warren, Scott's insane Kindred brother. Scott had been intended as the blood match for him but preferred to go on the run on account of Warren being a total psycho.

She smirked. "I bet Warren was furious when Dolores escaped."

The girl lifted her hand to her cheek. "Yes. He was."

The smirk faded from her face. *She must be going through all kinds of hell.*

"Can I ask you a question?" She had no idea how long Maggie would take. If she planned a quick bath before coming to get her, she'd likely find her dead.

Lucy didn't say anything but she waited.

Lexi turned her arm slowly. "Why can't I see my scar anymore?"

The girl narrowed her eyes, perhaps suspicious of a trick. "I don't know. I can't see anything either."

"And I can't feel him." She heard her voice tremble.

"The link is broken. Maybe—" The door opened again and interrupted her.

"I told you not to talk to her. I told you to simply get it done."

Lucy jumped in fright at Warren's voice. "But she said—"

He pushed her back toward the door. "Get out. I'll do it."

The girl ran out. Warren thrust his arm at Lexi and she darted to the side and into the cubicle after she released a shuriken which had been hidden between her fingers. The hand dryer exploded off the wall behind where she had stood.

She stuck her head out cautiously, half expecting it to be blown off. Warren pulled the shuriken from his neck. Blood pumped out as he dropped the spiky metal throwing star on the tiled floor, where it landed with a ping. He held his hand up to his neck and stared directly at her as the blood leaking through his fingers stopped.

Slowly and with an exaggerated motion, he drew a sword from his dimensional pocket. Lexi imagined that the long scimitar was supposed to intimidate her, but the sword was so long that drawing it out took several seconds longer than it should have and seemed almost comical.

"That's a long one." She chuckled. "Are you compensating?"

Warren's face settled into a cold mask. "I planned to do this quickly but now, I'll take my time so I can tell Scott how you begged and cried."

"Oh, my God. What are you? A Bond villain? Do you get paid by the hour or what?" She tossed another shuriken but he was expecting it. The little star careened away and struck one of the mirrors on the wall beside him.

Her adversary took one step toward her but froze when a bolt drilled through his neck. He writhed as he made choking sounds.

"You still favor the pistol crossbow, then." Lexi watched as her Kindred brother Isaac stepped out of a cubicle, followed by Maggie. "There's more of them outside. His name's—"

"We know who he is," he interrupted. "The mental fucker keeps turning up looking for you, saying you kidnapped his intended blood match."

Maggie stared at her. "Where the hell have you been?"

"I have so much to tell you. If it's worth it. It might not be and they'll probably simply counsel it out of your head again. I found things out about Kindred. Some really bad th—"

As she spoke, Isaac lifted his pistol crossbow and aimed it in her direction. Her words stuttered to a halt and she stared at it in disbelief.

He made a "come here" gesture with his other hand. "Lexi, move toward me. It's fine, but come to me."

"Hi." Scott's voice behind her made her shriek and turn.

Isaac loosed a bolt at the sorcerer, who flicked it away where he stood in a fae doorway. He stared at her. "I couldn't sense you. I thought you were dead." His voice trembled.

"I completely ran out of the good stuff." She raised her arm and winced in pain. "I couldn't sense you either. How did you find me if not through the blood match?"

"A common old locator spell with one of your socks."

"You're matched?" Maggie squeaked.

Lexi fixed her gaze on Scott. She'd never been so happy to see him. "This is Scott. Scott, Isaac and Maggie."

He waved awkwardly. "Hi."

"You're matched?" Maggie said again. "So *this* is Scott."

"Calm down. We're matched, not married. Listen, Zac, Mags. It looks like I don't need that lift now. But we do need to talk. I'll keep in touch. It was good seeing you." She caught Scott's hand, stepped through the fae door, and looked at them from the other side.

Maggie smiled at her, then looked at Warren. "Is he dead?"

Isaac checked him. "It looks like he's waking up, so he's not dead yet but could be soon."

He seemed to think about it before he fired a bolt into the bathroom door to alert those outside that things weren't going to plan. Then, he took Maggie's hand. The four of them looked at each other briefly before her Kindred siblings disappeared.

"I'd have let him die," Scott said bluntly and glowered at Warren, who opened his eyes. When he saw the sorcerer, the man flopped like a fish and stretched toward him.

Scott turned away. "Come on, let's go."

CHAPTER SEVEN

Scott and Lexi stepped out of the fae door into the garden of a little cottage.

Dolores was waiting for them. "Was that my old friend Warren?"

"Yes." Scott nodded. "Should I have killed him?"

"For the good of all mankind, probably." She patted his arm. "Don't worry about it for now."

Lexi looked around. "Where are we?"

"We're at my place and will return to Boulder City in a moment. We merely need to make sure you're safe when you're back in your world." Her boss turned to Scott. "Okay, do your thing."

"I'm trying. The magic's not going into her." He looked at Lexi's arm.

She looked at it too. "Can you still see the scar? I can't."

His gaze doubled its intensity as he stared at her arm. "I don't understand. It's not working."

Dolores nodded. "Okay. Shield her. We'll talk about it when we get back."

He put a hand on her head, then nodded.

Their boss opened her fae door.

Lexi looked over her shoulder before she stepped through. "Why don't we stay in your cottage?"

"The cleaner hasn't been in yet," the fae replied in a deadpan voice.

She narrowed her eyes. "That's not the real reason, is it?"

"No dear, it's not." The woman smiled, then sighed. "There's a limit to my protection. I already have Betsy and Todd in there."

"Aww! I'd have liked to have seen them." Scott frowned.

"You will, dear." She patted him on the back.

They walked through to a suburban garden.

Lexi gazed around at a soccer ball and a little pink bike lying outside the door. "Who lives here?"

Dolores opened the door and they entered. It was her little apartment, no longer a fishing shack near the lake.

They sat at the table and the girl retrieved the pouch from her pocket. "He dropped this."

"What is it?"

She handed the item to her boss. "It's the pouch the talisman was resting on in the museum. He went back to the museum for it. Should we leave it here for safety?"

The fae felt the material with her fingertips. She turned it inside-out and back, then handed it to her. "I think you should keep it with you and wait. If it's important enough that he came back for it once, he'll try again."

Lexi took it and winced.

Scott shook his head. "Let's fix your arm." He turned his chair to face her. She sat while he placed a hand gently on her arm and began to mutter unintelligibly.

After a minute, he looked at her. "You're all done."

She flexed her arm. It felt as good as new but when she looked into his face, she saw the concern there. "Yes?"

"Nothing."

"Say it." She was getting annoyed.

He frowned. "Your bone density is…different."

"Scott. I broke my fucking arm for the first time in my life. Do you think I haven't already figured that much out?"

"Sorry."

Lexi sighed. "No, I'm sorry. I'm not used to feeling so…" She wanted to say *scared* but chose not to. "Useless."

"Okay. Dick freaked out when you went missing. It's time to get back." Dolores went to the door. "We're back at the diner. I can't get us any closer with the wards."

She snorted. "Have you tried lately? We know for a fact that someone else is doing it."

Her boss grasped the handle and opened the door. "The wards are up now. I don't understand how it's happening. I'll have to look into it."

They walked through and Lexi looked around. She immediately noticed the truck driver again. He wore the same Raiders cap and plaid shirt and was seated at his table near the door, reading and drinking coffee. She was about to mention him but something more pressing was on her mind. "Is it my imagination or are we traveling an overly elaborate route?"

Dolores nodded. "Caleb knows you're both with me, so all of Kindred probably knows too. It's getting difficult to move around safely."

The fae turned to the man. "Thanks, Bill."

He looked up from his newspaper, smiled, and threw her a set of keys. "Take care, Dolores."

Lexi did a double-take. She was certain the guy had been there last time.

They left the diner, climbed into an old Honda, and headed to the condo.

The moment they entered, Dick leaped to his feet. "We thought you were dead."

Jesús walked into the room. "Mister Levin cried."

"I did not."

Jesús walked around the room, picking up glasses and tidying, but when he was behind his boss, he looked at Lexi and nodded his head as he mouthed, "He did."

Dick rolled his eyes. "I know what you're doing, Jesús."

"Yes, Mr. Levin." The man took the glasses into the kitchen.

"I wasn't crying. I'm allergic to the cheap fabrics in my condo. I'm allergic to so many cheap things—like that oxblood leatherette jacket you wear, Lexi."

She narrowed her eyes. "It's leather."

He looked pityingly at her. "I'm sure that's what they told you in the store."

"Fuck you."

"Fuck you too." The vampire put a hand on her shoulder. "Do you want coffee?"

Lexi nodded and patted his hand.

Dolores smiled. "It's so nice to see you two getting along."

A few minutes later, he was back with coffee. He put the mug in front of her.

She looked at him and nodded her thanks. Then she looked at Scott and extended her arm. "What's going on with me? Are we not matched anymore? Can that even happen?"

"I've never heard of this happening. I have no idea so I'll message Bryan." He took his cell out and began to tap it.

Lexi's stomach flipped. Her first thought was that she might see Bryan and she must be an awful sight. Then she remembered he was married to her sister and she sighed. "Great."

An hour later, he arrived and knocked on the frame of the open door. "Can I come in?"

Her heart lurched and she stomped on it mentally.

"Come in, Bryan." Scott shook his hand. "Anything?"

"I might have something. Well…it doesn't really explain why, but it might explain how…" He looked at them. "Here goes. As I said before, You and Ali were separated at a young age. The reason must have been because of what's happened now. When she's strong, you're weak, and when you're strong, she's weak. I think this gives us some good news too. I think this tells us you're a born legacy. You weren't made one by ritual. At least one parent must have been a legacy."

She frowned. "Why do you think that?"

Bryan crossed his arms and leaned back on the doorframe. "I think you're identical twins, so you started as a single cell with the legacy blood already in your DNA, then you divided into twins. That makes sense, right?"

Lexi looked away and mulled over what he'd said. "The fight with Alicia did leave me feeling ultimately weaker, but I hurled energy balls at the fae who killed Melvyn."

"You did?" Scott grinned.

"Yes. You're a crappy teacher. I blew a tree up."

The sorcerer gave her an incredulous look. "I haven't even taught you that yet."

"Exactly." She waited for a beat, then winked at him. When she turned to Bryan, he was frowning. "What?"

He grimaced. "That was probably residual magic. Whatever magic you had remaining in your system from Scott."

She clapped her hands and rubbed them together. "So, all we need to do is go to Alicia. I'll touch her for a few seconds and get my mojo back."

Bryan drew his brow down in a look of concern.

Lexi worried he would try to stop her. "I won't hurt her."

Quickly, he put a hand up to reassure her. "It's not that. I'm simply trying to work out the logistics. She's staying at the chief's house so there's always someone to look out for her." He thought for a moment. "Okay. I'll go back and I'll contact Scott when it's safe to come. You need to get out of Vegas so you can come immediately by fae door. We might only have seconds."

"Okay." She nodded. "We'll be ready."

Her gaze followed Bryan when he headed out the door and when she turned, the others were staring at her. Even Marcel was seated on his haunches with his head tilted and his gaze fixed on her.

"What?" It came out more aggressively than she'd intended.

Dick changed the subject. "So, what happened to the guy with the case?"

"I lost him, but he dropped this." She pulled the little pouch from her pocket.

"The talisman?" He looked delighted.

Lexi waved it. "It's empty."

The vampire slouched. "Oh. Never mind." He picked it up and examined it. She watched his face as he considered its relevance. "This is good, isn't it? Because he went back to the museum for it. If it's not important, why did he risk going back?"

She smiled. "That's the conclusion we came to."

"And he'd had the talisman for a couple of days before we arrived," he continued, "but he didn't start using it until he had the pouch. Oh… He needs this." He handed it to her with a grin on his face. "We don't need to find him. He'll come to us."

"Maybe it's not the talisman that's lucky at all. Maybe it's the pouch." She scrunched it in the palm of her hand.

With her fist closed around it, she wished with every hope inside her. "I wish I had my scar and legacy abilities back."

Lexi tried to create an energy ball. She looked at the others who stared pensively at her once again and shook her head.

Scott sat beside her. "After you disappeared, Dick went through the security footage of Mr. Dunk winning on the tables. He realized that the security guy from the museum stood in the background at every table Melvyn had played at. He held something in his hand but we couldn't see what."

She leaned down to stroke Marcel as he walked past. "Could it have been the talisman?"

"No, Melvyn had that." Dick picked Marcel up and kissed him on the head. "Jesús, would you take him out to do his business, please?"

Jesús took the puppy with a smile. "Come with me, little man."

"Melvyn took the chip out of his pocket a few times and kissed it," he continued. "In fact, every time he did that, Murder-Fae scowled."

"*Murder-Fae*. That's what we're calling him, is it? Well, it fits." She smirked.

Lexi scratched Marcel behind the ears as Jesús carried him past. "So Melvyn never was the lucky guy and you don't have to hold it to be the one winning. Interesting."

Dolores asked, "Where did the fae door lead to?"

"The first one led to a forest. Man, it stank like stagnant death."

Her boss sighed. "You shouldn't have chased him."

"I thought he'd been in a connected room. I flew around the corner and was through it before I knew what had happened. I chased him, threw the energy ball that blew the tree up, and when he escaped through another door, I launched myself through it behind him but he got away. That's how I broke my arm. God, that hurt."

Dick put a hand up. "May I ask a question?"

Everyone looked at him.

"What if that energy ball had killed him? How would you have gotten back?"

"Well… Oh!" Lexi shrugged. She hadn't considered that.

Scott was hesitant but asked, "What was it like seeing your f… unit again?"

She paused before answering. "I've spent the last year demonizing them all in my head, but Maggie and Isaac were simply

Maggie and Isaac. She was thrilled that we were matched and happy for me. What was it like seeing Warren?"

He ran a hand through his shaggy, blond waves. "I couldn't believe his face. God, what a mess. That poor mage. I regret not taking the time to kill him. I hope they didn't get to him in time. It would save lives in the long run."

"His face?" She frowned in confusion.

"Oh, you wouldn't have seen it." The sorcerer sighed. He opened his mouth, then closed it again.

Lexi could see he was struggling. "We don't have to talk about it if you don't want to."

"Do you mind if we don't? Honestly, I feel sick thinking about it."

They stood and headed to the cars.

She turned to him. "I'll need your help with something else. I can't get into my dimensional pocket. Everything's there—my money, cell phone, weapons…well, the good ones. I haven't lost it all, have I?"

"No, it's still there. I'll get your stuff out through mine." He sat on the back seat of Dick's car and hauled her gear out of his bag. She took a few items and rolled another twenty to hide in her vest.

Dick followed Dolores' vehicle out of town to the diner. They parked and entered, and she handed the keys to Bill, who remained at the same table.

The man didn't speak and instead, stared from the vampire to the clock on his wall. "My supe-dar says vamp but my clock says something else."

"Pleased to meet you. I'm Vamp Two-point-oh." Dick nodded at the man. "It's a little upgrade we're trialing."

Lexi rolled her eyes. "Could we have three coffees and whatever Mister Two-point-oh's having, please."

They sat with their drinks and waited to hear from Bryan.

"Maybe something's gone wrong. Should we call?" she asked when impatience finally won her internal battle.

"I'm not sure that's—" Scott was interrupted by a text message on his cell and he glanced at it. "We're up."

She rolled her arm and bent her elbow to ensure it wouldn't give her any more trouble. "How do you know where he is?"

"He gave us something to channel." The sorcerer opened his hand. A small pin with a police badge on it lay in his palm. He held it while Dolores put her hand on his arm.

The fae door opened into a bedroom with a single bed. Lexi looked around before she stepped through. They surmised this had been Alicia's bedroom growing up.

Scott was openly curious. "Huh. She has eclectic taste."

She glanced at him. "What?"

"The posters. She likes Linkin Park, The Black-Eyed Peas, and Leonard Cohen."

"That's weird," she commented as she studied the posters. They were the same as those she'd had on her walls.

The woman with her face lay asleep in the bed. Bryan stood over her and looked nervously from Alicia to the bedroom door.

Dolores put her hand on Lexi's arm. "I can't leave the door there. If there's another mage in the house, they might sense it. Call me and I'll come get you."

They stepped through and the portal vanished.

Bryan stepped back. "Let's get this done fast. The chief's just told me Caleb's coming over."

Lexi's face brightened. "That's useful. I could simply kill him now."

A voice came from outside the room. "Bryan? Is she awake?"

The man's face was a vision of shock.

His hand jerked out toward them when the handle on the

bedroom door turned. Suddenly, the two friends stood some-where else.

She spun in confusion. "Where are we?"

Scott ran a finger across a row of coat hangers. "I'd say we're in a closet."

Fortunately, it was a fairly spacious walk-in closet and they were surrounded by clothes, tools, weapons, and books. She stretched to open a drawer and a full-length mirror at the end of the little room clicked and swung open. They exchanged a glance and walked through onto a platform that overlooked what resembled a convention hall. The space was arranged in row upon row of booths.

"It looks like comic-con with no people," Scott said.

"I thought I heard you speaking."

Lexi jumped. Several large screens around the hall all displayed Chief Rand. He looked directly at the camera.

"She's not awake. I was talking to her anyway," Bryan replied. The view switched to the sleeping girl.

The sorcerer raised his eyebrows. "We're in his dimensional pocket."

"What? But it's huge. Mine's like a cupboard." She descended the stairs and he followed.

"It can look like anything you want it to. But I'll admit, I've never heard of anything like this." He looked as perplexed as he sounded. "Look at the signs. The booths are organized by year. Why would he do this?"

They walked past booths with pictures and screens on the walls while the conversation between Bryan and the chief continued. Lexi was drawn to one with pictures of a little girl. She recognized Brax-ton, the father of her unit, but he was far younger. Several pictures of a girl of about six playing with a doll caught her attention and she touched a screen on the wall. It immediately sprang to life.

The little girl was crying loudly and screamed, "I want Alicia."

Braxton stood nearby talking to a woman she didn't recognize. "This is horrible."

The woman stroked his arm. "It'll be okay. You know that sometimes, it can take a few counseling sessions to shift some memories. It's for the best."

The camera moved closer to the little girl and Lexi realized this was Bryan walking toward her. "Hi, Alexa. I'm Bryan. Look, here's Alicia." He placed a doll into the little girl's arms and she hugged it. Slowly, he sat on the floor beside her and showed her a toy truck.

Lexi wiped the dampness on her cheeks.

"Ah, Bryan." Caleb's voice boomed over the speakers and she went rigid at the sight of him grinning on the screens above.

Bryan nodded briefly and turned to Alicia.

"I'm sorry," Caleb continued. "I can't remember—have we met?"

Bryan took Alicia's hand and raised it to his face. "No… Well…" He suddenly appeared in the hall and stood at a notice-board at the end of a row of booths. He was there for two seconds, at most, while at the same time, he tucked his wife's arm under the covers. Calmly, he stood, turned to the visitor, and proffered his hand. "Kind of. We've spoken on the phone."

In the dimensional pocket, the two friends walked to the board with *Caleb* written at the top. Beneath were two columns for the things Bryan should and shouldn't know about the sorcerer. Lexi had the distinct impression that the man had tried to catch him out.

Caleb winced, then smiled. "Of course. Yes. How's our little superstar?"

"Did you see that?" Scott pointed at the screen. "Caleb's face? I bet that demon's still driving him crazy."

Chief Rand leaned closer. "We're keeping her in a magic-induced coma until we can find out what's going on."

The visitor continued to address Bryan. "Could you bring her out? I have some questions I'd like to ask her."

The young man paused before he answered. "Do you really need to? If it's about Cabo, we've completed our reports. But if you need anything about her fight with Lorenzo, I'm afraid I already counseled her."

Caleb smiled at him but his frustration could be sensed behind it. "Before she was debriefed? And why did you do that?"

"She was out of control and violent. I've never seen such ferocity and I assumed it must have been something Lorenzo did. I thought if she forgot it—I mean, that's why we have counseling isn't it? To protect us? But while it did remove the memories, it didn't work on her other issues."

"You were both told to stay away from Lorenzo."

"I didn't know she planned to do it but perhaps I should have guessed. She was upset when she heard about what he'd done to Thomas."

The sorcerer frowned. "Thomas?"

Chief Rand grimaced. "The vampire priest."

"Ah yes. That was most regrettable." Caleb sighed.

He leaned over Alicia's unconscious form and swept his hand above her. "Her bone density is almost double any legacy I've seen. And her legacy ability readings are off the chart." He grimaced and pinched the bridge of his nose, then turned to Chief Rand. "Kevin, may I use the bathroom?"

"Of course, you know where it is."

With a curt nod, he left the room

CHAPTER EIGHT

Caleb stood over the washbasin and his hands clutched the sides. Blood dripped from his nose onto the white porcelain.

What is the result of the experiment with the demon? Azatoth's voice was so loud in his mind that his eyes rolled back in their sockets and blood pulsed at his temples.

He had anticipated the question and attempted to lead with the good news. "The demon has fulfilled our primary purpose. It tried to escape by drawing a thinner from the demon realms, as we knew it would. We captured the thinner."

Azatoth hissed annoyance. *I know that. And the experiment?*

The sorcerer glanced into the bowl at the cascade of blood that now gushed from his nose. "As suspected, its body was strong but the mind is useless. It would not withstand your presence."

The demon paused before he issued his command. *Bring the girl. She will contain me. She will withstand my presence.*

Caleb pulled toilet tissue from the roll. "What about the sister? She's obviously been here. Bryan may know something."

Find out what the boy knows but let him live. I can combine my power with his air magic through their blood match. You are pathetic. You house a mere fraction of my mind within you and you crumble. Look at the mess you are.

He forced his gaze to focus on the mirror as Azatoth stripped the glamor he projected and he saw his true self. Most of his body was almost entirely riddled with broken capillaries in his skin. His eyes were bloodshot and his head was almost completely bald now. He had lost weight and jowls hung from his face. More than ever, he resembled a cadaver. It disgusted him and he looked away.

"The meteor storm is almost upon us. The conditions are favorable." Caleb's comment was met with silence. He looked unwillingly at himself in the mirror before he closed his eyes and drew a few deep breaths.

And clean yourself up. You're disgusting. His eyes flicked open as Azatoth's voice rattled through his mind. The demon laughed.

His movements slow and weary, he washed the blood from the sink and wiped it from his face with the toilet tissue, then flushed it. He took several more breaths to settle himself before he recreated his glamor. Soon it would be over, one way or another. He would either be rid of Azatoth or dead. By that point, he wondered if he cared which.

CHAPTER NINE

Caleb returned to the bedroom. He looked at Bryan and smiled again but this time, somehow looked more danger-ous. "Have you heard from Alexa recently?"

"Who?" The young man's vision flicked from him to Rand.

"Surely you know who Alexa is," the sorcerer pressed.

"I'm sorry. I haven't a clue." He didn't need to visit the hall for that one. It was obvious he shouldn't know who she was.

"Alicia's sister." He stared intently at Bryan and his face filled the screen.

"Her what?" Chief Rand interrupted. "I'm sorry, you're mistaken. She doesn't have a sister."

"Actually, Kevin, she has a twin, and coming into contact with her is the only way Alicia's abilities could have increased like this. It also means the other girl is now very weak. The council has kept them apart to stop this from happening." He looked at the sleeping woman.

In the pocket, the two friends glanced at each other. Lexi felt relieved to have their theory confirmed.

"So if we get the other girl back here, it might fix this?" Kevin sounded hopeful.

"Sadly, not at the moment. Alexa is a problem. She absconded from Kindred a year ago."

The chief's eyebrows reached his hairline. "She left? I've never heard of such a thing."

"It gets worse," Caleb continued. "She then seduced a young mage away from his family and from his intended blood match, a young man who is beside himself with worry."

Scott snorted.

"Now, she seems to be on a vendetta against the organization. We think she opened the portal in Palm Springs and attempted to murder me in Cabo."

Bryan looked from one man to the other. "But what about Ali? How can we help her? Can't we track this woman?"

"Clearly, the sister's after her. Perhaps she was in collusion with Lorenzo. She might have encouraged him to go on this evil, murderous rampage." Caleb shook his head as though he were genuinely sad. "We must keep Alicia safe. There's a place—you may have heard of it—Emmersley House. It's kind of a spa. She'll be protected there."

"You're taking her away?" Her husband sounded nervous.

A whirring noise started in the dimensional pocket. Lexi jumped and whirled. Her hand fumbled instinctively for her katana but she dug herself in the hip. "I really miss that pocket."

"You'll have it back soon," Scott assured her.

They stepped to a printer and watched a document print out of Emmersley House and Spa, followed by a picture of Caleb with his hand in Alicia's hair. They looked at the screens to see that it mirrored what happened in real life.

"Gross." Lexi shuddered and turned away. She stepped into an aisle and studied the booths on either side.

Scott stepped beside her and did a double-take "You're right. You did have the same posters."

She looked at the pictures of her old bedroom. Sure enough, it displayed the identical pictures.

He scratched his chin thoughtfully. "Maybe you're psychically linked with her."

"Maybe." She didn't think so, however.

They continued to walk.

Her companion looked into a booth while she wandered up an aisle. She came to the end of the row and a black, metal door with a sign that read *Bad Stuff*. Lexi put her ear to it, sure she could hear something on the other side. She moved her hand cautiously to the handle.

Chief Rand's voice drew her attention to the screens. "Maybe you should get out for a while. Have a walk around the Quarter. Sitting in here isn't doing either of you any good and you know they like to see us out there doing our job."

Bryan guffawed. "Are you sure about that? I've had very strange looks from the witches and shifters I've seen, and I mean more strange than usual. They want to know why we left them without support when Lorenzo went crazy."

Kevin patted his shoulder. "There was nothing you could have done about it. It was chaos in Palm Springs and your investigation in Cabo was important. For God's sake, someone tried to kill the head of the Kindred counsel."

Bryan turned to the sorcerer. "I'll come with her though, right?"

The man smiled his insincere smile. "Of course. I'll get her settled and we'll arrange a replacement unit to cover you here. You'll follow within a couple of days. I promise." He clapped his hands together briskly. "That's agreed then."

The young man looked at him, his expression wary. "I don't understand why she has to leave. If Ali's even stronger now than she was before and that means the sister's weaker, surely she can't be in danger from a powerless ex-legacy. It doesn't make any sense."

"Let's get a picture of that address." Scott started to retrace his steps and Lexi turned hesitantly away from the curious black door. They reached the printer and he picked up the sheets of paper lying in the tray. His cell phone appeared instantly in his hand and he took a picture of the details.

Caleb shook his head. "Bryan, you're a clever young man."

His tone drew their attention and they walked closer to a screen.

"That's a very good point," the Kindred leader continued. "I should have thought of it myself." He stretched his hands to the other two men at the same time and placed one on one each of theirs.

A slam drew the attention of the young hideaways. It was the door they'd entered through on the platform above. Alarmed, they looked at each other and hurried to the stairs. They both slapped their hands over their ears as hundreds of shutters descended over all the booths. One clunked over the printer as they moved past it. The screens changed to a black background with a red digital five-minute countdown.

Lexi lowered her hands as the sounds echoed and faded around them. "What the hell is going on?"

"I think Caleb's counseling him. I don't understand why the shutters—" As Scott spoke, the image and words vanished from the sheets of paper in his hand. "Oh."

They reached the top of the stairs. The door to the walk-in closet was clear glass from their side. Lexi was about to push on it when their adversary appeared in the room on the other side and they froze.

He looked around and poked through a couple of drawers before he pulled a copy of *Playboy* out, flicked through it, and shoved it back. With a smirk, he flicked a glance at the mirror door, half-turned, then looked again, directly into her face. Her heart hammered in her chest as he walked toward it.

She clenched her fist, ready to punch through the glass.

The sorcerer stopped about a foot from the glass and straightened his tie. With an inward sigh of relief, she realized he saw only himself in the mirror. He tapped at the floppy fat under his chin, turned, and disappeared.

Breath exploded from Scott in a panicked exhalation. "I didn't know it was possible to gain access to another mage's dimensional pocket without their permission."

Lexi was confused. "Dolores got into mine."

"She has permission because she puts things in there for us and I trust her—and I don't stash Playboy magazines in there."

"Really?" She smirked. "Where *do* you stash them?"

He rolled his eyes and led the way into the large area once more.

She looked around the hall and her gaze settled on the blank papers in his hand. "I don't understand this. I've never heard of objects vanishing from a dimensional pocket because someone's been counseled."

Scott raised an eyebrow. "How would they know?" He slid the blank sheets into the printer tray.

Startled by the question, she stopped and gaped at him. "Oh. Fair point."

He smiled. "I think you're right, though. We only use ours as storage."

"Yes…for teddy bears," she teased.

"And candy wrappers," he retorted. "Bryan seems to have this connected to his memory. Honestly, it's genius. The paper is an object but what's stored on it is a memory."

They stood and watched the screen as it counted down. At one minute to zero, the counter turned green and the shutters began to rise. Lexi wandered to a booth and pointed to a photograph of a book. "Hey, this is my favorite series—*The Belgariad* by David Eddings."

She touched the screen and it sprang to life. Alicia threw the book, which hurtled toward Bryan and he caught it. "Look, I'll take it back. I only thought you might like it."

Alicia, who looked about eighteen, pointed at him. "I feel like you're trying to turn me into someone I'm not. I don't even like fantasy and who the fuck is Leonard Cohen? Stop putting posters on my walls."

"I don't want to look at this stuff anymore." She stopped the screen and led them to the printer again. "It's supposed to be private." The truth was, she didn't know what to make of it.

The countdown reached zero and a beep sounded. Bryan appeared in the hall on the platform at the top of the stairs where a huge button had appeared on the wall with *stop alarm* written on it. He pressed the button, then froze when he noticed the two of them. Scott stepped in front of Lexi and she rolled her eyes.

The other man shook his head before he walked down the stairs. "Sorry. It takes a few seconds for things to come back."

Lexi looked at the screen. He was also in the bedroom, staring at the empty doorway.

When he reached the bottom of the stairs, he went directly to the printer. "Why was I counseled? That memory hasn't come back." He picked the blank sheets up.

"Caleb told you he's taking Alicia to recover at a spa," Scott explained.

Bryan flicked through the papers. "Caleb was here? I don't see the printout."

"Sorry. I saw it before the shutters came down, though."

"Shutters?" The other man looked around the hall.

"All the booths and the printer were sealed behind roller shutters."

"Ah! That makes sense. I've never been in here when it happened. That's interesting." He looked around. "I apologize if you've seen anything embarrassing. I panicked and didn't know what else to do." His gaze shifted to the door which read *Bad Stuff*.

Lexi wished she'd had time to open it. "We watched a video of me ugly-crying my eyes out. You gave me a doll."

"That was the day you joined us." Bryan turned to Scott. "Do you remember the details about where Caleb wants to take Ali?"

"I took a picture of it." The sorcerer took the phone from his pocket and showed the other man the photograph.

Bryan looked at it and the printer whirred to life again. A photo spewed from it of Scott's screen with the details from the note. He picked it up and they followed him to what appeared to be the most chronologically recent row of booths. He stopped at the noticeboard marked *Caleb* and he pinned the picture to the wall. The board was sparse. "As you can see, there's barely anything here, yet."

She raised an eyebrow. "I have a whole stack of information for you about him. When I get my abilities back, maybe I could set something like this up and send it over."

He narrowed his eyes as though he wondered how that might work. She suspected she'd given him a new project to work on.

"Did you know Caleb was in here?" Scott asked.

The other man froze. "In *here*?"

"Well, in the walk-in closet up there." He pointed.

Bryan exhaled sharply. "That's what it's there for. I've suspected for a while that the more powerful mages might be capable of peeking in our private spaces, so I keep weapons and spare clothes there and a few things that make it look like it's where I keep my secrets. The idea is that they hopefully won't look any further."

Lexi smirked. "Yes, he saw that too."

He blushed.

They walked along the row to the entrance. She tried not to look at the booths—it felt even ruder because Bryan was there with her—but she drew to a halt when she saw a picture of herself perched over Alicia with her katana. She gazed at it in horror before she looked away quickly.

It made her think about why she had attacked the girl so violently. "Why did she stab Scott?"

"When I got her home, she was raving about a doppelgänger and a sorcerer trying to kill her. She thought she was acting in self-defense and it was purely instinct. Let's get your legacy abilities back. Maybe Caleb won't take her away if I can convince him this extra strength has simply worn off."

Lexi looked at the two mages. "Will it disturb her when my magic leaves her?"

Bryan shrugged. "No, she'll stay asleep until I wake her." He turned and she realized with some surprise that they had returned to the bedroom. The two friends stood in front of the bed and Bryan was seated exactly where he had been during Caleb's visit.

"Where is she?" He stood.

They all stared at the empty bed.

"He's taken her already?" Lexi turned to Scott.

The other man looked at the wall. "The posters have gone. Everything's gone. He doesn't plan to bring her back." Bryan's face had turned white. "When I first came into the hall, I wasn't thinking about her at all. He'd taken her out of my mind completely. Now, I have to pretend I don't remember her. Oh, God, not again."

She looked at him, surprised. He seemed more annoyed than anguished.

Scott typed rapidly on his cell. "I'm messaging Dolores. We'll get on this immediately and will find her."

Lexi could think of nothing to say. She found the disappointment overwhelming. When the fae door appeared, she pushed to her feet and hurried to it.

"We'll let you know as soon as we know something," was the last thing she heard Scott say before she stepped through.

In the diner, Dick took one look at her face. "Shit!"

She tapped her hip nervously where her dimensional pocket should have been. "Caleb arrived and took Alicia. He said he would take her to somewhere called Emmersley House."

The vampire tilted his head and he frowned. "Emmersley…" he said as though the name resonated.

Scott stepped through and heard her explanation. "Should we go after him in your current condition?"

She turned to him. "He has my sister. It's very clear from what he said to Bryan that the excuse he gave for taking her was a lie. I can still wield a sword and fire a gun. I'll be fine. Of course, I'm not happy about feeling so weak. Maybe I should start on the vamp blood again."

Dick stepped away hastily. "Don't look at me. My contribution was involuntary."

Dolores waved a hand and her fae door vanished. "It wouldn't work anyway. Without access to your legacy abilities, you're essentially a regular human. They don't get superpowers from vamp blood." She slapped Scott's arm. "Are you looking for pie again? Everywhere you go, it's pie, pie, pie."

He dragged his gaze away from the menu. "Sorry, but they make amazing pie here."

"If you want amazing pie, I'll take you to Phil's Cornerdown Kitchen sometime. Or maybe not. We don't want you to die of longing."

Scott fixed his gaze on her and smiled. "Die of longing? Where is this place?"

"It's in a corner dimension of its own. People have been known to sit and die because they didn't want to eat anywhere else."

"What does he make?"

"Meatballs in Can't-Feel-My-Face sauce, Wings with Fuckno dip. The usual."

The sorcerer's eyes glazed over. "I have to try it, Dolores. You need to make that happen."

She checked the time. "Right, focus. You head to Vegas and get packed. I'll look into the fae who killed Melvyn."

"Can we help?" Lexi wondered if she would ultimately be

squeezed out of the team. She knew that shouldn't be her first concern, but she couldn't help the feeling that she was losing who she was, piece by piece.

Dolores sighed. "I'll look for answers in Fae. You head to Emmersley House. I'll prepare your background and arrange your flights."

She stared at her. "We don't even know where it is."

Dick's brow wrinkled in puzzlement. "That name sounds so familiar."

The fae stared at him. "It's in Maine."

Scott nodded to her. "You know it? Cool."

She looked at him with an odd expression. "I'm surprised you don't."

He grinned at Lexi. "This place must be famous. I wonder if we'll meet any celebrities."

They left the diner and climbed into the SUV. The sorcerer sighed. "When we get there, I want a last dip in the pool."

Dick turned in his seat to look at him. "You have something important to do, remember?"

"Oh, right. Well, after that, I'll jump in the pool."

Lexi massaged her temples. "I'm going to lie down." She wasn't even curious about whatever they were talking about.

Jesús came to meet them when they approached the condos. "Mr. Levin, the furniture has arrived. They asked what to do with what they were removing. I told them to pile it at the management company's offices."

Dick grinned. "You did the right thing. Wait, did you tell them to set it ablaze?"

"No. But I let Marcel pee on that nasty couch."

"We shouldn't teach Marcel bad habits but I think you're heading for a bonus this year, Jesús."

The man jumped up and down and clapped enthusiastically.

The vampire turned to Lexi and Scott. "Come and look at my

new furniture. I can't wait to see what Jesús went with. He's so close to that bonus."

Jesús looked sideways at him and led them in. "This way." He sounded nervous.

The entrance hall now had a large brass gong hung vertically in a wooden frame with a mallet on a bracket at the top.

Dick looked at it. "Bold. Very bold."

Scott's gaze fell on it. "That's perfect."

"You think?" The vampire's face brightened. "Onward, then."

They moved into the living room. His eyes narrowed slightly as he looked around.

"I chose to go with mostly Florence Knoll Bassett," Jesús explained hastily. "Her lines are clean and understated. The corner sofa is a statement piece. White would have been preferable, but this is a rental, after all, and you can't always guarantee quality guests. This and the credenza work together beautifully. The Rennie Mackintosh Italian Ash dining table and chairs, while matching well with the colors, contrast playfully with the Knoll in style." He took a deep breath.

Scott put his hands on his hips. "You're very knowledgeable, Jesús."

The man grinned with pride. "Mr. Levin has been paying for my college degree in design."

"He can't be a house boy forever, and he has a keen eye." Dick nodded as he looked around the room.

"One thing, though." Scott pointed at the gong. "Can I borrow that?"

The vampire looked both wary and confused. "Erm…sure."

Scott picked the gong up in its frame and took it through the front door.

Dick and Jesús looked at Lexi.

"Don't ask me." She shrugged and followed. When she reached him in the kitchen, he'd put her weapons on the kitchen counter but there was no sign of the gong. "Where is it?"

"It's in my dimensional pocket. I have some work to do on it." He sat and closed his eyes.

She retrieved her weapons and trudged up the stairs. Standing in the doorway of their room, she looked at the two beds, hers closest to the door and window to protect Scott. She sneered and wondered if she could even protect him now or if he might have to risk his life to protect her. The thought made her cringe inwardly.

Lexi walked into the master bedroom and dropped onto the bed. Her mind revolved through everything she didn't want to think about—all the unanswered questions. Seeing Mags and Zac had confused her. Bryan had confused her. Her stomach had done flips from the moment she knew he was alive, but it looked like he might have tried to turn Alicia into her? Now the possibility that he might want her existed, she realized she didn't want him at all. Not that it mattered.

What use am I to anyone?

Irritated, she straightened and realized she needed to keep busy. She closed the door, took her jacket and vest off, and hunted for more places to hide weapons. After an hour or so, she dropped the blades she'd been unable to fit in the clothes onto the bed. She threw the garment onto the pile, stretched beside it, and drifted off.

CHAPTER TEN

Lexi woke to "Mr. Blue Sky" from Dick's cell downstairs.

He answered in moments. "Hello, Dolores… Upstairs resting, I think. Would you like me to check? Tomorrow? Excellent."

She listened to silence for a while.

"Good heavens, no," he continued. "Don't book *me* into cattle-class. Book me first-class and invoice my accountant. Oh, yes. I'd forgotten I need to choose a surname. I'll mull on it for an hour or so. It's an important decision, you know. I've had the same name for a hundred years… Yes, I'll let you know tonight. Do the others need new identities? Let me choose Lexi's, please. How about Mary-Beth, or Mary-Jane? Something with a hyphen… Oh, very well. I'll update Scott." After a moment he added, "Marcel, walkies."

Just when she thought Dick was a decent guy, he'd start being a dick again. She rolled her eyes. He was mostly a nice guy and he would give you the monogrammed shirt off his back but sometimes, he could be utterly thoughtless. She turned over and lay quietly for a few minutes before she opened her eyes and sighed. Moping was pointless. She decided to get ready for dinner.

At that moment, the ruckus broke out.

The sound of a crashing cymbal echoed around her. The air shimmered in the room and Murder-Fae appeared with a nasty grin on his face. He held an evil-looking curved knife but didn't approach her with it. Her gaze shifted from the knife to his face and she scowled belligerently. She'd fallen asleep without her vest on and the moron now stared at her breasts.

Scott teleported into the room. He raised his hands, no doubt to perform a spell, when he also noticed that she was bare-chested and froze momentarily. The fae tapped the mage's forehead and he was suddenly nowhere to be seen.

Lexi looked at the intruder in horror. "What have you done?"

He glanced at the floor and moved his foot. She edged slowly onto her knees and looked over the end of the bed to where a tiny Scott waved at her from the floor.

The fae hovered his foot above him. "Give me the pouch or your boyfriend's floor jello."

She put her hands up, clasped them around the back of her head, and simultaneously arched her back a little. "Please don't hurt him. I'll do…anything." She noted that the creep's gaze darted between her face and breasts.

"Just…just give me the pouch." He continued to look, though.

"It's in my vest. Do you want me to take it out?"

"No! Pass the vest over slowly." He seemed to sense that she was up to something.

"Fine, okay. Look, I won't try anything." She leaned sideways with her one hand still at her neck and the other stretched to reach the vest.

He sneered at her. "I know you won't try anything. The word's out that you're a total dud—no abilities, no nothing."

How in the hell would he know that?

Her face flamed with the shame of his words but she picked the vest up with a finger and thumb so he could see she only intended to pass it to him. She kept it far away from her body and swept it in a slow arc, hoping Scott had the sense to run from under the guy's foot.

"Take it. And here I thought there was nothing to learn from those Vegas magicians."

His gaze flicked to her face and inevitably, to her breasts. "What does that—"

She acted as fast as her half-naked, total-dud body could move.

"What does that mean? Let me answer that for you. Misdirection. It means that while you gaped at my girls here, I was able to slip a blade from under my vest with my toes. And while you stared over there at the vest and here at my breasts, I passed that blade to my hand and was able to stab you through the head with it."

"Lexi." Dick stood in the doorway. "Why are you talking to the dead fae?"

"We were having a conversation. I see no reason to end it simply because he died while I still had a point to make."

A hurried glance at the floor revealed Scott coming out from under the bed. She picked him up gently and placed him on her hand.

"Get Dolores," the tiny sorcerer yelled.

Lexi put her ear closer to him. "What?"

He tried again. "Call Dolores. Do-lor-es."

Dick knelt beside the fae's body and began to search through his pockets. "He's asking you to call Dolores."

"Oh, I know. I can hear him perfectly well." She smiled at Scott. "But he's so adorable this size. Can't I keep him like this? I've heard the teacup human line before, but it's never been this literal."

The vampire looked at Scott, who was seated in her hand with his head in his hands. "I suppose you could get a little cage with a wheel so he could exercise and a Barbie to talk to."

He scowled at Dick and made a rude gesture.

Lexi straightened on the bed. "Oh, my God, that's so *cute*. Did you see? He flipped you a teeny-weeny bird."

Dick chuckled, then held up the golden poker chip "Tadaaa!" He threw it on the bed.

She gave him a thumbs-up and focused on her friend again. "Now, Scott. We need to talk. It's about breasts. These are breasts, see?" She held him at breast height. "They are not a reason to lose focus and get yourself killed—or shrunken. Do I have to walk around topless until you get used to them?"

He put his hands over his eyes and shouted, "Put them away. They're really big and it's freaking me out."

The vampire leaned against the wall and raised his hand. "Excuse me. I'm impervious. May I be excused from class?"

Lexi nodded. "Yes, would you mind calling Dolores?"

"Roger that." He nodded and walked away.

She returned her gaze to Scott. "I'd also like to point out that while Dick had his strength and speed—"

"I was walking the dog," he interjected from downstairs.

With a sigh, she continued. "And you had all your powers to hand, I was the dud with no legacy abilities but I was still the kickass bitch. I *am* still the kickass bitch and I will always be in this team." She thought for a moment. "Unless you count my breasts as a superpower. And to be honest, I do lean in that direction."

Gently, she placed Scott on the bed and pulled her vest on.

She glanced at the talisman. "Hey, see if you can use that to regain your regular size."

He crawled across the bed to the chip. When he was almost there, she moved it six inches further away. He stopped and stared daggers at her and she giggled.

The sorcerer reached it and sat on it. He scrunched his eyes closed for a moment, then opened them. "Nope. Are you sure this is the right one?"

Lexi considered the question. "Maybe it's because I'm holding the pouch and I'll be honest, I'm not one hundred percent invested in your request. Try asking for a pitcher of margarita to appear on the dresser."

Scott scowled at her.

She picked him and the talisman up as Dick appeared at the door

He stepped into the room and closed it behind him. When he opened it again, Dolores stood there in her apartment. "You're lucky. I've been out of cell range and I was about to head out again. I happened to turn back for something when my phone rang."

Lexi raised an eyebrow. "Hmm. That *was* lucky."

Dolores went to the French doors on the opposite side of her room and opened them. "Quickly." She gestured urgently to Dick.

He yanked Lexi's blade from Murder-Fae's brain, picked the corpse up, and ran through the apartment at vamp speed and up the boardwalk. With little compunction, he threw the fae's body into the lake.

Lexi carried Scott to Dolores and looked through to the lake beyond the doors. "I hope no one discovers that body any time soon."

A series of splashes drew their attention and the vampire looked over the edge and grimaced. He hurried to the portal. "Alligators."

Dolores raised her eyebrows. "Really? I've never seen alligators there before." She turned to Scott and tapped his tiny head gently. He outgrew Lexi's hand and she dropped him but before he had the chance to fall, his growth had covered the distance. He stood with an angry look on his face. "Thank you, Dolores." He turned to Lexi and shouted, "Yes, I know you have breasts," before he stormed to the bed and sat with his arms folded to stare straight ahead.

The fae looked from one young person to the other and shook her head. "I won't ask. I need to go before they put the wards up again." Dick stepped out and she pulled the bedroom door closed.

Two seconds later, the vampire opened the door again with a flourish to confirm that Dolores' apartment had vanished, and he bowed dramatically.

Lexi clapped.

Scott put his hand out to Lexi. "Talisman and pouch, please."

He dropped the talisman into the little bag. "A pitcher of margarita," he said acidly.

Dick looked around. "That's disappointing."

The sorcerer put a shielding spell on the items and handed them to Lexi. "No one will be able to track this now. I suppose you want me to get rid of the blood."

She looked at the floor. "If you don't mind."

He stood over the blood with his hands outstretched.

The gong sounded and the blood remained where it was.

Dick raised an eyebrow. "Whoever's messing with the wards must have realized he's not coming back." He wandered out of the room.

Lexi glanced at her friend, then at the floor. "You did offer."

"Fine." Scott stormed into the bathroom and returned with a scrubbing brush and a bucket of hot water. She blocked his path at the door and took them from him. "Go for a swim. You deserve it."

After she'd scrubbed for a few minutes, Dick appeared at the door. "What on earth are you doing?"

"Getting the blood up."

"Stand aside, sister. I'm an expert in all things blood." He took the bucket and brush into the bathroom and returned with the bucket refilled and a bottle of hand wash in his other hand. "This needs cold water." He rolled his sleeves up, squirted the hand wash onto the floor, and scrubbed with the cold water. She went to the bathroom and retrieved a towel. When she started to kneel, he stopped her.

He put his hand on her shoulder. "I've got this. You empty the bucket."

Lexi tipped the bucket to empty the contents down the sink, refilled it, and squirted bleach in.

I miss the zombie twins.

She paused at the sound of singing and returned to the room to find Dick standing barefoot on the towel while he shimmied across the floor.

"Blame it on the Bossa Nova." He looked up. "Oh, Lexi. I learned this technique from Jesús. He's a little genius."

Scott shouted, "Lexi, Dick," from downstairs as they finished. She went into the bathroom and squashed the towel, pink with blood, into the bleach.

They headed downstairs to where the sorcerer stood in the hallway with a pitcher of margarita. "Look at what I won at the pool bar."

Lexi pushed her plate away. "If I die today, it'll be with a happy stomach." She looked at Scott who appeared to be seated in front of an elephant graveyard. Huge, stripped white bones piled on the two plates he'd cleared in Jessie Rae's.

He put his hands on his stomach. "It's with great sadness I have to announce that as much as I'd like to, I cannot possibly manage a third plate."

Dick raised an eyebrow. "I'm sure the local cattle wranglers were holding their breath."

She grinned and passed the talisman to Albin. "What will you do with this?"

The man held the little pouch in his hand. "I can't thank you all enough for this. I can't put it on display yet. It will probably simply get stolen again."

Scott put his hand out. "Keep it somewhere safe. It's shielded so they shouldn't be able to find it, even with the wards down. If you decide it's too hot to handle, call Dolores. I'm sure she'll be able to put it somewhere safe."

Albin shook his hand. "I'm about to see Dolores anyway. She has asked me to help her with something. Then, I'll work out where to keep it."

Lexi stood and, although she intended to shake his hand, she somehow hugged him instead. He kissed her cheek and she sat again, a little dazed.

She smirked when Dick stumbled awkwardly to his feet.

The historian turned to him, took his face in his hands, and kissed him for a full minute.

Unable to help herself, she leaned forward and stared, her elbows on the table and her face in her hands. "I wish I was Dick's lips." She grimaced. "Did I say that out loud?"

Albin broke away. "And I'll see *you* when you're next in town."

The vampire swayed on his feet. "I'm not leaving. I live here now."

"Call me." Albin chuckled and turned and walked away.

Dick took his cell phone out and fumbled with it.

Lexi leaned across and took it out of his hands. "Not now. Show some restraint. Call him tomorrow."

He frowned. "Are you sure? I mean, have you ever actually dated anyone."

She stared at him. *I am a calm pool of tranquility.*

"Yes, you're right." He put both palms on the table. "I'll play it cool."

To refocus herself, she checked on Marcel who was asleep under the table with his paws around a stripped beef bone that was roughly the same length as his body. She took the cell phone out of the satchel she was now forced to carry and snapped a picture of him to send to her boss. "I'm texting Dolores. Any messages?"

Dick straightened. "Oh, yes. Tell her "Bond." She'll know what it means."

Lexi had forgotten about his new name. "Bond, as in James?"

"Precisely." He smiled and she thought he looked quite smug.

She shrugged. "Okay." She began to tap the screen.

A few minutes later, her phone chirped. "She says our flights are booked for twelve pm tomorrow. Tickets and extra documentation will be in a sealed envelope at the information desk."

The vampire smiled. "Perfect."

Lexi refused to allow an evil little giggle to escape her lips.

Scott straightened abruptly. "Something's wrong."

They focused on him and waited as he rifled through his bag.

He withdrew a sheet of paper and stared at it.

She waited a whole two seconds before she asked, "What's that?"

Dick peered around the sheet. "Is that a fax? How retro."

"Yes. I asked Dolores to put the machine into my dimensional pocket. It's a message from Bryan."

Lexi took it and read it aloud. "To: Scott, From: Bryan, Subject: Urgent. Message Reads: Caleb has returned, I think—" She flipped it but it was blank on the other side. "Where's the rest of it?"

Scott had his cell in his hand again. "I'm messaging Dolores. We need to get to New Orleans. It'll take too long to do it in jumps."

Jesús stood on the sidewalk, waiting for them. They pulled up and Dick passed the sleeping puppy to him before they accelerated away.

Twenty minutes later, they were at the diner outside the city and Dolores was waiting for them. "I don't have long. It's taken me this long to secure a meeting with the elders."

They hurried through the fae door and stopped outside Chief Rand's house.

She looked at her watch. "I'll be back in a minute."

"I'll look around back and see if I can peek through any windows." Dick stepped to the side of the house and made his way toward the rear.

Scott turned to Lexi. "Can you stand out of view of the door? Your face might complicate things."

Lexi nodded when she realized he might be right. She stood at the side of the house while he knocked on the door.

It opened and a man spoke. "What do you want?" He was abrupt and sounded hostile.

The sorcerer responded in his best polite tone. "May I speak to Bryan, please?"

"Bryan? There's no Bryan here. You have the wrong house. Get out of here." The door slammed.

He tried knocking again.

The door flew open and the chief shouted in his face. "What?"

"I'm sorry. You might remember me—I was helping Alicia with her car."

"I told you, you have the wrong place. I don't know any Alicia. I'm busy and I have to get this done. Leave me alone." The door slammed again.

Scott wandered to where she waited at the corner of the house. "Well, that was weird. Caleb must have counseled him to forget Alicia and Bryan. I'd say it looks like he doesn't plan for either of them to return. The chief was really angry."

Lexi turned to him, her expression grim. "As angry as Mayor Todd was when Caleb sent him to burn Dick's house down?"

They stared at each other.

Dick appeared. "The kitchen window was open. The house stinks of gasoline and a woman is simply sitting there, staring into space."

"Shit!" the two friends said in unison.

"Get him out of there." She turned to Dick. "The wife."

Scott disappeared and a moment later, a loud whomp made her freeze in concern.

Dick vanished in the next moment.

Dolores's door arrived at the end of the yard a second before Scott appeared with Chief Rand unconscious in his arms.

Lexi looked around as the front window exploded. "Was Bryan in there? And where's Dick?"

The sorcerer disappeared again and returned with Mrs. Rand and Dick. Without a word, he was gone again.

Dick spun and hurriedly extinguished a few flames on his jacket. "I thought I was a goner. I tried to get her out, but she put some mage whammy on me and I couldn't move."

A few seconds later, Scott returned. He coughed and shook his head. "He's not there."

They stared at the blazing house for a moment before Dolores called her door. "We need to get them out of here." She frowned. "Where to?"

Lexi thought for a moment. "Joseph's bar."

Scott lifted the chief in his arms and Dick threw the man's wife over his shoulder. The fae put her hand on Scott for directions as she called the door. They stepped through into the courtyard at Joseph's bar.

He walked out to them. "Is that the chief of police?"

"Hello again, old friend." Dick put the chief's wife on a table. "It is."

The sorcerer laid Kevin on the next table and stood with his hand on their heads. "I've counseled both of them. They shouldn't remember anything, but they may still have the compulsion to kill themselves. I don't know enough about the magic that caused this."

Lexi turned to Joseph. "I'm sorry to dump this on you. Bryan and Alicia have been taken."

The man nodded. "Go. We've got these two." He looked at the unconscious form of Chief Rand. "The War of the Blood has begun."

She stared at him, both confused and alarmed. His words resonated in a way she couldn't quite grasp.

Dolores turned to her and opened her fae door. "I need to return to the Hall of the Elders. You get to Vegas and prepare for your flight. I'll try to keep you updated."

Lexi faced her. "What aren't you telling us? Why do you keep swapping how you travel? And why are we flying tomorrow?"

The fae sighed. "I think I'm being tracked by the Elders. Something's not right."

Dick was at her side in a moment. "What can I do? Do you want me to stay with you?"

She shook her head. "You can't come to fae."

The vampire rolled his eyes. "Bigots." He looked around. "Scott, then. Or what about Joseph? You'd go, wouldn't you Joseph?"

Dolores put her hands onto his chest. "I'm fine. Calm down. You have to go. Look after each other."

They returned through the door and walked to the car. As Lexi climbed into the passenger seat, she considered everything that had happened. "What's changed?"

Dick glanced at her but didn't respond. He and Scott waited.

"Caleb's known the chief for years—and presumably, Bryan and Alicia." She looked at the two of them. "Why is he burning his bridges now?"

The sorcerer looked out of the window as the car began to move. "It feels like something is coming."

At the condos, they reached the door as Jesús stepped out to walk Marcel. Dick took the lead from him. "Don't worry about that. I'll walk him."

He released it and watched as Dick strode along the sidewalk with Marcel bounding along beside him. "He's changed."

The comment so eerily echoed her question in the car that she did a double-take. "How so?"

"For a man with many years to fill. He seemed so empty

before. He's always been kind to others." Jesús chuckled. "In his own way. But I think now, he's starting to be kind to himself."

Lexi looked at the young Mexican man. "Goodnight, Jesús."

She thought about what he had said. There was no denying it. Dick was a complicated man. She suddenly winced as she remembered the childish trick she was playing on him and realized she had begun to regret it.

I hope he's feeling kind tomorrow.

CHAPTER ELEVEN

Erika stood in line at her local convenience store.

The woman ahead of her was flustered. She turned and apologized for about the ninth time. "I'm so sorry. I know my wallet is here somewhere."

She smiled kindly. "There's no need to hurry, I'm fine."

As she watched, more of the woman's hair slipped out of the knot on her head and made her appear bedraggled. It was clear her head wasn't in the game. She had started by asking for a scratch card, then put her groceries through, then asked for a scratch card again.

"Here it is." The woman yanked her purse out and paid for her groceries. She put her change away, then looked at the two tickets. "Oh. I didn't mean to buy two." She turned to Erika. "I'm sorry I kept you waiting. Here." She thrust one of the tickets into her hand. "Good luck."

The shopper moved to the end of the counter to start scratching her card.

Erika paid for her sandwich and moved to the end of the counter. "Any luck?"

She shrugged. "Not today. How about you?"

It made sense that she might as well scratch the card before she left the store. If she was lucky enough to win ten dollars, she'd have to come back to cash it in.

When she felt in her pocket for a coin, the woman handed her what appeared to be a poker chip.

With a smile, she took it. "Who should I thank if I win a million?"

"I'm Dolores," the woman responded with a smile.

Erika scratched the silver coating from the boxes. Ten dollars, four million dollars, two dollars, ten dollars, four million dollars, two dollars, five dollars, one dollar. She looked at the last box. She could win ten dollars, but most likely two dollars, if anything. After an inward shrug, she scratched.

"Erika? Are you all right?" Dolores stared at her. She held her hand out and the girl wondered if she wanted the ticket back.

Instead, the woman plucked the chip from her fingers. "It's my lucky chip."

"Am I— Sorry, what?" *Did I tell her my name? I guess I must have.* She looked at the card and counted, then counted again. Finally, she checked the instructions. It was the same figure three times. Four million dollars, three times.

When she looked up, Dolores had gone. After a moment, she refocused on the ticket, then stuffed it into her bra. She left her lunch on the counter. While she loved her job and loved the people at Emmersley, she decided not to work today.

CHAPTER TWELVE

Lexi turned away from the information desk with a large envelope in her hand.

Scott looked at the time. "We'll have to run to make this flight." He stared at Dick.

The vampire rolled his eyes. "I said sorry."

"Seriously, dude. How could you forget you had a dog?"

"He's my first dog ever. I didn't know I couldn't pop him under my arm and bring him along. I'm sure I've seen the Kardashians do it."

"The guy said it depends on the airline," she explained. "Some allow pets in the cabin. Unfortunately, we're traveling with an airline that wants to throw dogs into the cargo hold."

He was outraged. "Over my dead body."

She snorted. "So much is wrong with what you said."

Scott shook his head. "Poor Jesús was halfway back to Palm Springs when you called him to collect Marcel. What did he say when you called the second time and said not to bother?"

Dick grimaced. "He'd already arrived at the condo. I told him to stay there and drive back the next day. Do you think Marcel's okay?"

They walked quickly as they spoke. "He's fine. He was asleep on the couch in front of the tv last time I checked."

Lexi raised an eyebrow. "It sounds like you've expanded your dimensional pocket."

"I put Marcel's basket in there and stuff to keep him amused. Dolores put a few things in there for me this morning."

They approached the check-in desk, which had two lines. One had a long line of customers and the other was empty with a *Business and First-Class* sign.

"Well, this is me. See you at the other end." Dick walked ahead and down the left side to the counter.

Scott turned around, "Where's he going?"

She rolled her eyes. "He booked himself into first class."

"I suppose if you can afford it." He shrugged.

Lexi folded her arms and looked at him. "Would you do it?"

He appeared to give the question serious thought before responding. "No. Not if my companions couldn't afford it."

"Exactly." She shook her head. "Keep watching. This will be fun." *I hope.*

"Oh no." He looked sideways at her, his expression horrified. "What have you done?"

Dick removed his passport and boarding pass from the envelope and handed them over. The woman on the check-in desk gazed at the passport, then showed it to her colleague who glanced at him. Her lip twitched.

The vampire stiffened a little and adjusted his shoulders. He was obviously uncomfortable.

"Thank you, Mr. Pick. Have a nice flight."

"Mist— Thank you." He took the documents and stepped away from the desk. His face unamused, he opened the passport and flicked his gaze to Lexi before he strode through the gate.

She guffawed.

Scott gaped. "Mr. Pick?"

A smirk settled on her face as she waited.

Her companion's jaw dropped. "Oh, my God! Dick Pick—you changed his name to *dick pic?*"

They moved forward in the line while she almost cried with laughter. "I needed that."

He frowned, slid his passport out of his envelope, and paused nervously before he checked it. "Shaun Green. That seems normal." He exhaled sharply with relief.

Lexi checked hers and showed it to him. "Lena Hearne."

They boarded the plane, where an unhappy cabin crew waited for them. They apologized and moved to their seats.

Scott grinned as they hurried through the aircraft. "On the bright side, everyone's already seated so we don't need to wait to get to our seats."

"Yes, but look—they also hate us because they should have taken off ten minutes ago."

He looked at the faces of the people they passed. "Oops."

A young uniformed man stood at their seats to help stow their gear. "You're lucky you were traveling with a first-class passenger. Otherwise, they would have simply left."

They sat hastily and buckled in.

The sorcerer looked out of the window and then at the screen in front of him and pressed a few buttons.

Lexi stared at him. "Can you calm down?"

He grinned. "I've never been on a plane before."

She nodded. The excitement was one she could identify with as she'd only been on a plane once, just before she met him.

"I need to check on Marcel." Scott closed his eyes.

Idly, she wondered if Marcel was in his dimensional pocket peeing on the chihuahuas. She had a thought and poked her companion. His eyes flew open. "Don't let him anywhere near my swords or knives. If he loses an eye, Dick will probably try to kill us."

He nodded and closed his eyes again.

The cabin crew completed their safety routine and the plane taxied to the runway and took off.

Scott had seemed to be in a trance but the moment the seatbelt light went off, he bolted out of his seat. "I need to go to the bathroom."

They walked to the back of the plane and Lexi stood outside the bathroom. At a sudden bark, one of the cabin crew looked suspiciously at the door. After two more barks, she hurried away.

Lexi kicked the door. "Keep the noise down in there."

When Scott emerged two minutes later, three crew members waited. They looked into the cubicle as he left.

"Is there a problem?" he asked.

One of the women was still suspicious. "What was that barking sound?"

He smiled broadly at her. "Oh, the alarm on my phone went off. It sounds like a dog barking. It's hilarious isn't it?"

She gave him a withering look and marched away.

Lexi slid into the cubicle. "You'd better have cleaned up if you had a dog peeing in here."

One of the crew laughed and she smiled before she locked the door. The smile dropped from her face and she began to examine the seat.

When she returned to their seats, Scott had settled into the window seat again. "Did you manage to get him to go?"

"Yes. But I had to conjure a little patch of grass. He was a very good boy but he's lonely in there, so I'll have to sneak off for a while. Can I have the chicken and a bottle of water when they come to take orders?" He waited for her to nod, buckled in, and closed his eyes.

A few minutes later, the phone under her screen rang. She picked it up. "Hello?"

"That wasn't very funny," Dick said.

"Really? And Mary-Jane is?"

"Oh. You heard that." He coughed. "How's Marcel?"

"He's okay. Scott took him to the bathroom and no, don't ask. He's gone in with him now. They're probably playing fetch. What about you? Are you stretched out and drinking champagne?"

"As a matter of fact—" The vampire sounded brighter.

Lexi scowled and hung up.

Two flights and seven hours later, they arrived at Portland airport in Maine and met in baggage claim.

Dick's case had been the first one through and the others had only carry-on luggage, so they headed out quickly.

She looked at his suitcase. "At least you're not traveling with that ridiculous trunk."

"Of course I am. Scott's carrying it." He turned to the sorcerer. "How's my baby?"

"Snoozing. I gave him the chicken from my meal on the flight."

When they stopped at the first gas station, Scott took Marcel out of his dimensional pocket.

Dick opened his arms and the dog leapt into them. "The poor little guy looks traumatized."

"You know how animals usually travel," Lexi muttered. "He had it good."

After the puppy's walk, they climbed into the car.

She stretched on the back seat. "Has Dolores sent you any further information about this facility?"

Scott turned in his seat. "Only the location. All we know is it's called Emmersley House and Caleb said it's some kind of spa."

"Emmersley House. That still sounds so familiar. Perhaps it's a world-class spa—that would explain why I've heard of it. I could use a good massage."

"Dolores will text us our cover stories," the sorcerer continued. "She's already told me I'll work as a physiotherapist."

Lexi thought about that. "Maybe we should stop somewhere for dinner and go over the details before we get there."

Dick swerved the car. "Nope. That's a no. You're not to even look at it. We won't go in as staff members. I absolutely will not give foot massages to people with questionable hygiene. We'll go in as guests and that's the end of it. Scott, I'll buy you a back, sack, and crack. And Lexi, I'll buy you a facial." He looked sideways at her. "For both your faces."

Scott looked from one to the other. "We can still stop for dinner, though, right?"

They drove slowly through the town and drew into the parking lot of a bar called The Red Lion, which was styled on an English pub. The building was white with black beams, a nod to the British Tudor style. It was the only establishment they could see on the main street that appeared to still be open and serving food. They entered and the only other customers they could see were several elderly people seated together at a table. The locals stopped speaking and looked at them suspiciously before they returned to their drinks.

Lexi chose a table at the back and they sat and took the menus from the center of the table. She ran her fingers down the options. "I don't even recognize half of this stuff."

Dick raised an eyebrow. "It's British-themed so I assume this is British food." He glanced at the options. "Good heavens. They have faggots on the menu." He leaned back, folded his arms, and stared at her.

She looked up. "What?"

"I'm waiting for you to tell me to run for my life."

"Don't be silly." She shook her head.

He smirked at her thinly veiled disappointment.

Scott glanced at the vampire between picking condiments up and studying them. "Have you ever been to England? The real one?"

"Yes, a few times. I entertained the troops during the war.

Bing and Bob went to the South Pacific and I went to South Birmingham. I've been a few times post-life too, but I've always flown cargo in a crate. You think standard-class is bad. At least you can watch movies and drink bourbon."

Lexi felt a twinge of guilt for the trick she'd played on him and for the way she'd judged him for traveling first class.

The sorcerer tapped her arm with the menu. "Do you know what you'll have?"

She glanced at the menu again. "I think they've taken this English-themed food a little too far. I'll play it safe...chicken pie maybe."

The waitress came to the table.

Scott looked up enthusiastically. "I'll have faggots, chips, and mushy peas, please."

Dick looked at Lexi. "The gauntlet has been thrown down."

She looked at the menu again.

The vampire took the opportunity to place his order. "I'll have two double bourbons, no ice."

"I'll have..." She lifted her head. "Toad in the hole with bubble and squeak." She placed her menu down like a winning poker hand. She and her friend looked at each other, neither sure who had won.

The waitress didn't look at all fazed by their strange requests.

After she had left, Dick looked at them. "Do either of you know what to expect on your plates?"

Scott grinned. "Not a clue."

Lexi shrugged.

The drinks arrived. Dick took one bourbon and tipped it into the other.

One of the people at the other table stood. He looked the worse for wear and stumbled around chairs and tables as he headed toward the *Bathroom* sign.

When the food arrived, they looked doubtfully at their plates, then swapped.

They had finished eating when the door banged open. The waitress had been setting cutlery out on the tables and jumped with fright.

A heavy-set, angry-looking woman with a silver whistle on a chain around her neck entered and looked around the room. The people at the other table immediately fell silent.

She delivered a stare at the elderly people, so frosty that it made Lexi uncomfortable. "I might have known," the woman snapped.

The two ladies at the table slumped and groaned. The man gave the angry newcomer a drunken wave. "Hi, Nila. Come and have a drink." He slapped his knees as though offering her a place on his lap.

"If I don't see you in the back of my car in ten seconds—" She spoke coldly and gritted her teeth.

"You'll what?" asked the drunken man. "Y'old sourpuss."

The woman glanced at the waitress but didn't seem to notice the others at the table at the back of the room. "We'll talk about that later."

Lexi was shocked by the menace in her voice.

The two ladies stood immediately, although it seemed to be a struggle. One of them negotiated a somewhat shaky path to the door with two walking sticks and the other shuffled along behind her. The man stood and finished his drink. She suspected he was being deliberately slow. He joined the others at the door and the three elderly patrons filed out in silence. As they exited, the woman took her whistle and blew hard, and the lady with the sticks wobbled in fright.

Instinctively, she grasped Scott's hand. They didn't have the link anymore but she knew him well enough to know that he was about to jump to his feet. The door closed. His face was outraged.

Dick shook his head. "Well, she's a piece of work."

The waitress who had stood nearby returned to collect their plates. "She scares the crap out of me. What a dragon."

The vampire smiled. "I think that comparison might be unfair to dragons."

She giggled and blushed under the gaze of his topaz eyes.

Lexi made a mental eye-roll. *What is it with him and waitresses?*

The bathroom door opened and the man who had gone in there about a half-hour earlier stumbled out. He looked around the room when he realized his friends had left. He wove to the waitress. "Ahh, feck it. I fell asleep, Gina, and they abandoned me."

The old man's musical Irish accent was appealing.

Gina smiled at the old man. "You dodged a bullet there, Patrick. Nurse Ratched turned up."

He sighed. "Jeez, I'd best start walking then. Here's hoping my hip doesn't fail me before I get there."

The girl patted him on the shoulder. "I'd give you a lift to Emmersley but I have another two hours here."

Dick turned in his seat. "If it's Emmersley House you're going to, we're about to head there if you'd like a ride."

The man's face became guarded. "And who might you be?"

"We're weary travelers about to check in there." The vampire held his drink up encouragingly.

Patrick chuffed a laugh. "I can guarantee that you're nowhere near as weary as you'd need to be to get into there."

Dick pushed the fourth chair at the table out. "Would you like to join us for a drink? Patrick, is it?"

"Well, if you'll give me a lift, it would be rude not to." The man sat and proffered his hand. When he looked at him, his brow creased. "You look mighty familiar."

The vampire's face brightened immediately. "Well—"

Lexi kicked him under the table.

He shrugged and gave a tight-lipped smile. "I've been told I have one of those faces."

The newcomer leaned forward and looked at each of them. "So what will you be doing at Spandau prison?"

Lexi fixed him with a confused look. "Span what?"

"Kids!" The old man rolled his eyes.

"Spandau was a German prison," Dick explained. "It was famous for housing Nazi war criminals."

Patrick grinned. "An educated man. I like you already."

Scott mumbled, "This place sounds less and less like a spa."

The vampire turned to him with a disgruntled look on his face. "It might be time for you to check that message from Dolores."

After a quick nod, he scrolled through his phone, then held it out so Lexi could read the message with him. She sighed and deflated. "It's not a spa. It's a residential care facility for elderly and convalescing supernaturals."

Dick slapped his palm to his forehead. "Now I know why I recognize the name." His shoulders slumped.

Scott's jaw dropped. "No. No, it's a spa. Caleb said it's a spa."

She raised an eyebrow. "I believe his exact words were 'a kind of spa.'"

"But a residential home isn't any kind of spa." He looked utterly despondent. "Not even a little."

Patrick looked at them all in turn, his eyes narrowed. "Now that we've ascertained that you're not spa guests, who are you?"

The vampire sighed. "I don't even know what my cover is and it's already blown."

Lexi kicked him again.

He brushed his pant leg with his hand. "Would you please stop kicking me? This is a thousand-dollar suit."

The old man's eyes widened. "Cover? You're investigators? I'm confused. When that guy from Kindred visited, he said there was nothing to investigate and told Maisie to stop wasting your time."

Scott exchanged a look with her, then turned to Patrick. "We're not Kindred. I'm Shaun, this is Lena and Richard. Can you tell us why you called Kindred?"

He gestured to the waitress. "Gina, could we have a last round before we go—and one for yourself."

His voice lowered. "It was my friend Maisie who reported that two of our friends had disappeared. We were worried about reporting it to Kindred because they own the place now. But who else do we turn to? Something's not right there. Maisie said she could trust the Kindred team from her local town, so she made the call. Then she went missing too."

"When did the disappearances start?" Lexi asked.

"A month ago. The last one was…" His voice caught. "Maisie, a few days ago."

Scott took his cell phone out and tapped quickly. "And how many?"

"Three residents. But you're not here because of that?"

Lexi shook her head. "It's likely that your disappearances are connected to our investigation, though. Did they start happening after the change in ownership?"

Patrick nodded excitedly. 'Yes. About a month after. We had great hopes when we heard about the buy-out. The place has needed a few repairs for a while. Then we learned it was Kindred who took over, sticking their big nose in where it's not wanted again."

Scott paused his finger over his screen. "Can you give me details? What exactly happened?"

"A couple of my friends disappeared in the night—a week apart with no notice and no goodbyes. Just gone. Nurse Ratched —that's Nila, who you had the pleasure of seeing this evening— said they'd moved back with their families but neither of them had any family to speak of. Maisie was much more vocal about it than I was. She suddenly went to live with her son in Australia a few days ago but I know she doesn't have a son in Australia. She doesn't even have a son, period. I haven't said a word about it since I'm terrified. We all are."

They stopped speaking while Gina put the drinks on the

table. Lexi took a sip of hers and decided to risk a question specific to their case. "Have they brought any new residents in over the last day or so?"

He paused, clearly thinking. "None that I'm aware of."

"And how about construction work?" Dick asked. "Is anything going on?"

Patrick shook his head. "But it's a bloody big building with large land around it."

"Have you seen any Kindred other than your local unit?" The last thing she wanted was to run into Caleb before she had her legacy abilities back.

"They've visited a few times, but I haven't seen any sign in the last few days. They might not be staying in the main house. There are a couple of lodges on the grounds."

She leaned forward. "I assume that while we carry out our investigation, we can rely upon your discretion, Patrick."

He responded with all sincerity, "Of course. But can I ask—who are you? I've never heard of Kindred being investigated by anyone. In my experience, they act with impunity and we simply suck it up."

Lexi and Scott flicked a glance at each other. She felt ashamed and she guessed he did too.

"I'm a sorcerer—"

"Let's get up to the house," she interrupted hastily. "It's getting late." She didn't want to hear how Scott would describe her—or worse, if he stumbled over his words or was unsure. If he said she was a legacy, she'd feel like a fraud, and God forbid he'd introduce her as a normal human. How humiliating. She shuddered inwardly.

Soon, I'll find Alicia and get my abilities back and I'll never complain again that I'm a dud.

Lexi wondered if getting her abilities back meant never seeing her sister after that. She shook the thought away. One problem at a time was more than enough to deal with.

CHAPTER THIRTEEN

The car eased between large iron gates and wound slowly around a tree-lined drive to the house. It was late and the only sound was the crunch of the tires on gravel. Scott gazed out of the window. "This place is huge."

Patrick nodded. "It sure is."

They parked at the side of the main building and walked toward the entrance.

The old man smiled. "Now, if you don't mind distracting young Stuart on the night desk for me, I'll sneak past."

Lexi chuckled. "You're a rascal. I'll have to watch you."

She entered through large glass doors with Scott and Dick. A small desk was situated on the side of the lobby and a young man was seated behind it. He tried to balance a pen on his forehead. When he noticed them, he fumbled to right himself and opened his mouth to speak, but his attention was drawn down the hallway. "Oh no. Not again."

When the clerk's attention was diverted, Lexi glanced over her shoulder to where Patrick darted from the door to duck behind the stair rail and start climbing.

Satisfied, she looked in the same direction as the clerk. A door at the end of the hallway burst open and an elderly, naked gentleman shuffled through, swinging a pair of underpants. It was the drunken man from the pub and he was singing. "Look for the bare necessities—"

Lexi looked down and smirked. "I think I found them."

The old man let the underpants fly and headed through the front door.

The clerk glanced at Lexi, then looked at Scott. "We cool?"

The sorcerer cleared his throat without looking at her. "Yeah, we're cool."

She stood in silence while he placed his pen down and stood. Her shoulders drooped. "We cool" was something supes said in front of humans to ascertain whether or not it was safe to reveal their supernatural nature in their presence.

Belatedly, she wondered if she should have tackled the old guy but a man in white and holding a robe pushed through the door and raced after him. He was followed a moment later by another man, also in white, who ran through the door, saw the three of them, and slowed to a walk.

The clerk pointed at the door. "They're fine. Just go."

He shifted—or, rather, his bottom half shifted. The man was a satyr and now raced away on his goat legs. He picked up speed and continued through the front door.

When the clerk stepped out from behind the desk to retrieve the underpants—now hanging from a large potted plant—it was evident that he too was a satyr.

Dick muttered, "I'm remembering more and more of the things I've heard about this place."

Lexi glanced at Scott, who picked up a brochure titled *Emmersley House Residential Care Home, Senior Living and Rehabilitation*. He flicked a final glance at the instructions from Dolores on his cell.

The clerk stepped behind the desk and returned his attention to the three of them. He smiled as though they'd only now walked through the door and nothing whatsoever had happened. "Hi, I'm Stuart. How can I help you this evening?" His gaze darted toward the door the absconding naked man had fled through and returned to the three of them.

Scott took the lead. "I'm Shaun Green and this is Lena Hearne. We're here with Mr. Richard Pick. You should be expecting us?"

"Hmm?" Dick glanced up from the brochures. He stepped to Lexi and asked with his voice lowered, "What exactly is our cover?"

She shushed him.

"Yes. Mr. Pick. I'm afraid we were only notified of your transfer earlier today. We're still organizing your room downstairs." He continued to read the notes, then looked at Scott. "Are you certain he's no longer a risk to himself or others?"

The vampire's whispers into her ear became more insistent. "What have you done now?"

"This is all Dolores," she responded quietly but impatiently. "I haven't a clue. You'll have to ask Scott when he's done." She glanced up the stairs to where Patrick lingered to listen to the conversation.

"Absolutely. He's only here to recuperate and is no longer delusional." Scott smiled at the guy, turned his smile to Dick, and tried to shrug discreetly.

At the word "delusional," the vampire's eye began to twitch.

Stuart looked from Scott to Lexi and passed two room keys to the sorcerer. "Your two rooms are ready. You'll be in the old servants' quarters on the top floor. The rooms there are quite small so I hope they're okay for you. Most of us are local so we only use a couple of the overnight rooms here for standby shifts. The top floor hardly gets used at all, so you'll have it almost to yourselves. It's unusual for a resident's personal staff to stay here, though. He must have some pull."

Dick smiled. "Oh, I couldn't survive without Shaun and Lena. You know, you could always give me a room upstairs too."

Scott turned and stared hard at him before he smiled at Stuart. "He's kidding."

The clerk looked dubious. "Are you sure he's cured?"

The sorcerer nodded confidently. "That's what they tell me." He turned to the vampire. "You don't think you can walk in the sun anymore, do you, Richard?"

Dick's jaw worked as he fought back the instinctive response. "The malaise has left me. I only need a little rest."

Lexi looked at Stuart, who studied the new patient with discomfort.

Stuart narrowed his eyes. "He's...erm, lowered his pointy parts."

She swung to face the vampire, who stared dead ahead with his fangs bared. Her first instinct was to pull her foot back to kick him but she stopped when he turned and stared at her. Dick could look quite dangerous sometimes and this was one of those times.

"He hasn't eaten," Scott said quickly as the vampire retracted his teeth.

The clerk raised an eyebrow. "There's a refrigerator in his room." He took two bracelets from a box, wrote on one, and passed it to Scott. "Put this on him, please. What are you—a mage?"

"No. I am a sorcerer, but I'm in Mr. Pick's employment, not Kindred."

He held the second wristband out. "You need to wear one too."

Scott passed the first band to Lexi, who held it out and stared at Dick. After a few moments, he sighed and extended his arm to allow her to close it with a click.

Lexi waited, then asked. "What about me?"

Stuart laughed. "Normals don't need one."

She blushed furiously.

Her thoughts clicked into focus after a second and she wondered why Scott would need to wear one. She opened her mouth to ask as he clicked the second bracelet onto himself.

Too late.

Stuart passed papers to him for signature. "What do you two do then?"

The sorcerer handed each sheet to the man as he signed it. "I'm Mr. Pick's physiotherapist."

Dick stepped closer to the desk. "Shaun is a gold-star masseur. I would absolutely die without my daily massage."

The front door opened and the two white-coated care assistants—both had fully shifted and displayed goat legs and horns—entered with the elderly man, who wore the robe.

Stuart called out to one of the men. "Josh?"

The other man tightened his hold on the elderly man. "I've got him. Come on, Albert. If you're good, I'll get you some candy."

"I only went out to give my candy cane a little air." Albert cackled.

The assistant chuckled and shook his head as he led the elderly man through the lobby.

"Thanks, Raj," Josh called after them and headed to the desk. "Hey, Stuart. What do you need?"

Stuart waited until he was at the counter. "Is Mr. Pick's room ready yet?"

"Yes. We filled the refrigerator minutes before Albert made a run for it."

"He reeks of booze." He lowered his voice but Lexi could hear him quite well.

His colleague grimaced. "Yeah, Nila caught a few of them in a bar again."

Stuart drew in a sharp intake of breath.

The man rolled his eyes and mouthed, "I know."

The man focused on the computer, then looked at Scott. "Oh,

you *are* a physiotherapist. Dude, your qualifications are great. What a weird coincidence. We lost our physio today. She called in to say she won the lottery and she's not coming back."

"Wow! That's lucky." The sorcerer's gaze cut to Lexi.

"Don't you try to poach my masseur. I'm very attached to him." Dick stepped forward and linked arms with Scott.

"I wouldn't do that, Mr. Pick," Stuart assured him hastily. "I expect the position will be filled from inside Kindred."

When the vampire wandered away to leaf through brochures, Stuart turned to Scott again. "I've never met an independent sorcerer before. In fact, every one I've ever heard of has either been a Kindred mage or was training to be a Kindred mage."

He shrugged and looked around. "I've never been much of a joiner. We heard they'd taken over. To be honest, we half expected legacies to be everywhere."

"If they are, I'll turn around and get on the plane again," Dick interjected.

Stuart leaned closer and lowered his voice. "It was really quiet when they first took over but now, they're always visiting—well beyond the regulation weekly visits we've always had. They're a pain." He stood quickly as though he realized he'd said too much. "If you *are* a mage, I guess I'm in trouble now."

Scott smiled. "I've worked for Mr. Pick for several years and I have no intention to jump ship now."

He seemed satisfied. "Right." He looked at Lexi. "And what do you do?"

The sorcerer looked from Stuart to her and back again. "This is Lena she's his…nail technician."

The clerk stared at Lexi and she stared incredulously at Scott.

Dick stepped forward. "She's my donor. I prefer to be discreet on paper."

Stuart raised his eyebrows but nodded his understanding. "I see. You won't need the refrigerator, then."

Dick waved a hand. "Leave the refrigerator. I like a variety and sometimes, Lena's a little…sour."

She flushed and she had to bite back a caustic comment. "Right, let's get our stuff."

They stepped out and walked around the building. Back at the car, she thumped Scott's arm. "Nail technician?"

The vampire laughed and she spun and thumped his arm. "Donor? Really? And would you stop talking about your cover within earshot of strangers? Cover this, cover that. It's just as well you didn't get the name Bond. You're the worst spy in the history of spying."

He smoothed an eyebrow. "Well, after that dick pic stunt you pulled, if I'd thought faster, you'd have been my proctologist."

Scott chuckled as they retrieved their luggage from the car. Dick put Marcel on his lead and he jumped down.

When they returned to the lobby, Stuart looked at the puppy. "I'm sorry, we don't allow pets."

The vampire lifted his dog into his arms. "This isn't a pet. It's my therapy dog."

The clerk looked doubtfully at Marcel, who whined appealingly. "I'm afraid it's up to Nila. Don't get your hopes up, though."

"Stuart, why don't you leave that decision up to me?"

He scrunched his eyes closed for a moment.

Lexi turned to where Nila stood in the doorway with the silver whistle around her neck. The hairs on the back of her neck stood up and she had to force herself not to shudder. She didn't need her legacy abilities to tell her this woman was dangerous.

Nila approached with steady strides and Stuart took a step back. "Sorry, Nila. I was only—"

The woman spoke over him. "You must be Richard." Her voice softened. "I've been expecting you." She extended a hand to Dick.

Stuart's face showed shock at her changed demeanor. Almost instantly, he seemed to remember himself and set his face to neutral.

Lexi noticed immediately there was no "Mr. Pick." This woman considered herself his equal. It seemed at odds with her role as a service provider.

The vampire shook her hand. "Nila. What a pleasure to make your acquaintance. I see you run a tight ship here. Very impressive."

She watched his face. He knew instantly the woman was enamored. The playful twitch of his lip was masterful. There was nothing in his face that betrayed his true thoughts about this horrid woman and he looked, for want of a better word, entranced. She glanced at Nila and found her eyes disconcertingly icy, with pupils like tiny pinpricks. There was something overly shiny about her skin—something unhealthy.

"Is he house-trained?" the woman asked.

Lexi caught a whiff of her breath and had to clench her stomach muscles to stop herself from heaving.

"I'm sorry?" he replied like he'd forgotten there was a world beyond her face. "Oh, Marcel. Yes, most certainly. I run a tight ship myself."

Dick deserves an award for this. He is pure method.

The ghastly woman smiled. "Well, how about I show you and Marcel to your room?"

He followed her along the hallway. She stepped through a doorway and he glanced at Lexi before he continued.

Josh—who had leaned on the counter—straightened. "I'll show you to your rooms."

Stuart held a pen out to Lexi. "You need to sign in." She tried to take it but he tightened his hold on it. She fought a scowl when she saw his grin. He winked at her. "You know what they say—all the girls go satyr sooner or later."

She stared at him until he released the pen, then wrote her fake name in the register. Without a word, she dropped the pen on the counter and turned away.

The two friends climbed the stairs behind Josh. On the fourth floor, they turned down a myriad of hallways.

"Are we expected to find our way out of this place?" Lexi asked.

Their guide shrugged. "I know. Sorry. It'll probably take you a couple of days to find your way around."

Josh showed them to two oddly shaped rooms next to each other. They were small but clean. "These were the servant's rooms at the turn of the century. As you might guess from the circular outer walls, we're in one of the turrets now. You should find it peaceful. No one ever comes up here except to access the laundry closets and clean."

Scott looked out of the window into the darkness. "How old is this building?"

"There's been a structure on this property for hundreds of years. First, it was an old stone tower. That was about four hundred years ago. Over the years, the house replaced that, and new parts have been added by different owners ever since. It's kind of a warren now." He turned to Lexi. "I wonder if you shouldn't be in a room on the basement level with your boss." He laughed. "I know I like to be near the snack machine."

She stared at him and tried to keep her face blank.

These satyrs will be a pain in the ass.

Josh put his hands out in a gesture of surrender. "It was only a thought."

Scott looked at her. "You will not leave me here all alone. It's creepy."

The other man pointed out the small staff kitchen, lounge, and bathroom facilities. After they assured him they didn't need anything else, he left them without a backward glance.

Lexi threw her satchel and overnight bag onto the bed in her room and showered. She headed into the small kitchen and dining area. It didn't appear to see any use at all.

Ten minutes later, Scott wandered in with damp hair and looked around. "I don't like this place."

Dick appeared at the door, also with damp hair. "I am with you one hundred percent."

She scanned the hallway behind him.

The vampire walked into the room and looked relieved. "Don't worry. She left for the evening. I thought I would have to throw her out of my room."

"Her breath." She screwed her face up in disgust. "What is she?"

He shuddered. "I know. Thank God I don't have to breathe. I haven't a clue what she is. I've never come across anything so disconcerting before." He stepped to the door. "I'll go down to Marcel. I think she even spooked him."

Scott ran his fingers through his damp blond curls. "So, what *do* we know?"

Dick spoke from the hallway without turning back. "We know it's not a fucking spa."

CHAPTER FOURTEEN

Lexi ran through old abandoned rooms lined with rough stone. She reached a stone spiral stairway and started to climb.

"I sense you are near." The voice was raspy and seemingly everywhere.

The stairs seemed never-ending and the muscles in her legs burned. Someone or something behind her was gaining. She stumbled to the top of the staircase and a door that was locked. The rushing footsteps came closer. She put her hand out and averted her face, not wanting to see what was coming.

A scream made her turn. It was Scott. He stepped back, his face burned where her hand had touched it.

She bolted into a seated position in bed. Her body was slick with sweat and she shivered in the pre-dawn cool of her New England bedroom. She put her hand on her chest and breathed measured breaths in an effort to slow her heart rate before she slid out. Still a little on edge, she crept along the hallway toward the bathroom and past the servants' lounge. Movement caught her eye and she stopped, retraced a couple of steps, and looked in. Dick was seated at the window in the dark.

"When exactly do you sleep?" She yawned.

He turned to face her. "I only need a couple of hours these days, but I'll be in that basement all day. Did you have a nightmare? Your heart is racing like a charging rhino."

Lexi wondered if she should deny it. She hated to appear weak but she nodded. "Do you dream?"

"I used to dream every day that I was either playing tennis with Harv or lying next to him near a swimming pool in the sun. I haven't had that dream for a couple of weeks. I miss it." He sighed. "I would give up every future moment of this life for one last tennis game with Harv." He returned his gaze to the window and the darkness.

She stared into the blackness. "Can you see anything?"

The vampire shrugged. "I can see my reputation will be in tatters after this. Delusional indeed."

"Not *your* reputation. Richard Pick's, and he won't exist after we leave here." She coughed. "That was a stupid trick with the name. But under the circumstances, it might have worked out for the best."

"You could be right. And with regard to your original question, I can see everything but there's not much of interest to see." He settled into silence and she continued to the bathroom.

Outside her room, she hesitated and considered looking in on Scott but heard him snoring. She entered her room and switched the light on to orient herself.

Lexi noticed a strange mark on the bedsheet. She walked to the bed to examine it. On closer inspection, it wasn't a stain as she'd assumed but a burn mark in the shape of a hand. "What the hell?" She sat beside it, her mouth agape. The dream came to her and she placed her hand over the mark. It was a perfect fit. She pulled away quickly, pushed to her feet, and threw the covers off the bed to remake it with the burn tucked in at the bottom. Although she tried, she couldn't return to sleep.

Finally, she rose with the pre-dawn light. Dick had gone, presumably to the basement. She wandered through the hallways of the top floor, opened doors to rooms, and looked out of the windows for signs of construction activity on the grounds. The rooms along one wall had no windows other than a small skylight in the ceiling.

How depressing.

During her exploration through the rooms and hallways, she located a walk-in closet with paint cans, brushes, and dust sheets. She darted to her room, snatched the burned sheet, folded it, and shoved it at the bottom of the pile of dust sheets.

With that disposed of, she took another sheet from a laundry closet and remade the bed. She could hear Scott moving and by the time his head popped around the door, she was seated on her bed, sharpening a shuriken.

She glanced up. "Sleep well?"

He frowned. "I snored, didn't I?"

Lexi stood and glanced at the bed. She turned to face him. "I have no idea. I slept like a log." Lying to him wasn't usually an option but without the empathetic link, it was surprisingly easy.

They headed to the small staff kitchen and made coffee.

She sat at a table while he went through all the cupboards from one end to the other and inexplicably repeated the process.

As he opened and closed the doors, she questioned her actions. *Why didn't I tell Scott about the dream and the mark on my sheet?* She knew why. While she hated to admit it—even to herself —she was afraid of losing him or somehow being unworthy of his friendship.

Scott sniffed. "I've been through every cupboard in here. There isn't a crumb of food but I smell bacon. I suppose we'll have to go downstairs."

Her eyebrows raised. "You sound unusually reticent to get breakfast."

He took her mug. "I don't want to run into that Nila woman. She's really horrible." He shuddered to emphasize his point.

As though he'd invoked her, the penetrating sound of her

whistle pierced the air from a lower floor. His eyes closed as he exhaled sharply and this time, it was Lexi who shuddered.

She moved toward the door. "We need to start looking through this facility. If Alicia and Bryan are here, they're probably in danger. The longer this takes, the worse their chances are. I've had a look around this level and there doesn't seem to be much up here."

They walked cautiously down the stairs and as they rounded the staircase into the lobby, Stuart replaced the receiver and looked at them. "Hey, good morning. Would you like the tour?"

Scott grinned. "Will it start with food?"

The clerk laughed. He stuck his head around the door to an office behind him. "Karen, I'm taking Shaun and Lena into the breakfast room. Can you keep an eye on the desk?" He walked ahead of them but was still within earshot.

Lexi turned to Scott. "You and your stomach. I was looking forward to a tour straight away." She stared intently at him.

He smiled. "I thought it might be nice to meet the other residents and find out what goes on here…for Richard."

Stuart glanced at them over his shoulder and they both smiled at him.

Their guide led them into a room that was set up for breakfast with residents seated at tables, eating and talking.

Patrick's voice bellowed across the room. "Well, if it isn't my new pals. Come on. I'll buy you breakfast."

They made their way across the room to his table.

Scott shook his hand. "Good morning. How's your head?"

The old man winced. "It'll be better when I've got this down me." He pointed at a plate filled with sausages, bacon, eggs, and pancakes.

The sorcerer's stomach gurgled.

Stuart grinned. "I'll order breakfast for you, then come back in a half-hour or so. We can do the tour before I finish my shift. Do you want the same breakfast?"

They both nodded enthusiastically and sat at the table.

Patrick looked up. "And here comes Phyllis."

A lady in a purple leisure suit moved slowly through the room with a walker and joined them. Lexi recognized her from the evening before in the bar where she'd used walking sticks.

A young man followed her, holding an enormous plate of sausages, bacon, and eggs. He placed it in front of her as she sat. She nodded her thanks to him and rubbed her hands enthusiastically. "I love breakfast. It's my favorite meal."

The old man grinned. "But what about dinner, Phyllis?"

With absolute sincerity, she replied, "I love dinner. It's my favorite meal."

He passed the pepper to her. "This is Shaun and Lena. They dropped me here last night. He's a sorcerer."

The woman didn't look at them. Instead, she muttered. "You're living here now, are you? You only came a couple of days ago. I haven't gnawed on it since then." She waved her arm to reveal an identity bracelet similar to Dick and Scott's.

Scott looked confused. "We arrived last night."

Phyllis scowled. "I mean your other Kindred pals—or brothers and sisters or whatever you call yourselves."

Lexi looked at Patrick to confirm that he wore a band on his wrist too. Her brow wrinkled in puzzlement as she shifted in her seat to look at the other residents. Everyone wore them. It dawned on her that these bracelets—and the one she had fastened onto Dick's wrist—were more substantial than the flimsy hospital bands she'd seen in the past. She glanced at Scott's arm.

Why is he wearing one?

She glanced at him. He gazed pointedly at Patrick's breakfast. She tutted and rolled her eyes.

The old man patted Phyllis's hand. "Calm down. They're nice people."

"Rubbish." She groaned dramatically. "I bet Nila called them in. We'll be in trouble for leaving the grounds last night."

Scott dragged his gaze away from the food and looked at them. "Huh?"

Patrick lowered his voice. "They're secret investigators and are looking into the disappearances. They're undercover."

Lexi dropped her face into her palm.

Dick, so help me!

Her gaze bored into the old man.

He frowned. "Was I not supposed to say that?"

She leaned back when the food arrived and coffee was poured. As soon as the server had left the table, she explained, "We're not with Kindred. We work for a different organization."

Scott leaned closer and looked from Patrick to Phyllis. "What we're doing is dangerous. If it gets back to Kindred, we could be killed. I don't want to have to counsel you."

The woman's eyes narrowed. "I thought you said you weren't Kindred."

"That doesn't mean he doesn't know how to do it," Lexi muttered.

Patrick looked down, chastened. He looked so pathetic that she actually felt bad.

The sorcerer frowned. "I'm sorry to be rude but I don't sense anything at all from you or any of the residents, and I didn't last night in the restaurant either."

"We're all muzzled." The old man waved his bracelet. "These inhibit our supe natures, so we can't sense you and you can't sense us. They come once a week to make sure we haven't messed with them."

"One of you could be a goddamn vampire and we'd never know it," Phyllis added.

"Oh, they have a vamp with them too—a very nice chap for a vamp." To Lexi, Patrick added. "I happened to hear you in the lobby when you signed in last night."

She smirked. "Happened to hear."

Scott looked across the table at the salt. He opened his hand, then frowned. His eyes narrowed as he stared at the little bottle but it remained where it was. "My telekinesis isn't working. It's this." He began to tug at the bracelet.

Phyllis leaned forward and put her hand over his. "I wouldn't do that if I were you. You'll wake a week from now, drooling like a baby and wondering what hit you."

Lexi raised an eyebrow. "I was surprised when you put it on last night without asking why."

He shrugged. "I was so worried they'd know we weren't who we said we were, I wasn't thinking." He looked at it, horrified, but released it. "Why did they do this?"

Patrick tapped his band. "Only the staff are allowed to use their abilities. I don't mind it so much. Phyllis and I both have a touch of the Alzheimers. It's why many of us are here. When shifters get bad with it, we can shift at very inadvisable times. It's for our safety and others. A small price to pay."

The sorcerer looked puzzled. "Don't they let you shift to stretch the kinks out occasionally?"

He shook his head. "Neither of us has shifted for a couple of years. We probably never will again. Eat your food, lad."

"I'm sorry. I didn't know." Scott looked at his plate but ate as though he'd lost his appetite.

Lexi glanced toward the door. "So, what's Nila then? Some kind of demon, Anti-Christ, or what?"

"Aye, you'd think it." Patrick paused and sighed. "No one knows. We think she's a shifter, though."

"Why?" Scott asked,

Phyllis looked toward the closed door as though the woman might walk through it at any moment. She leaned closer and lowered her voice. "Because she's a cow."

The sorcerer snorted.

"So, have you any idea why Kindred has suddenly bought this place?" Lexi asked.

Patrick swallowed his food and glanced around before he spoke. "Emmersley has always been independent, but it's had a fairly civil relationship with Kindred as long as I've been here. Suddenly, though, some deal has been done and Kindred are the new owners. They promised the staff would be able to stay on with no changes, but then Nila turned up with her damn whistle."

Phyllis put her hand on Lexi's. "By all that's holy, I'd like to shove that whistle up—"

"Now, Phyllis," the old man whispered. "Don't get yourself worked up." He smiled at her and continued. "On Friday, almost all the office staff were fired. The only people still here are the kitchen and cleaning staff and a few care assistants. Apparently, they're hiring from within Kindred."

Scott looked up from his screen. "Weren't the staff suspicious that people had disappeared?"

The woman shook her head. "The staff insisted there was nothing suspicious going on after Maisie contacted Kindred. A guy came a week later—not one of the usual ones who check on the bracelets. It was a loud-mouthed, rich-looking man called Caleb Deane. He didn't seem very interested in the disappearances at all. He went into her room and later, she'd completely changed her tune. She said we were wrong and shouldn't make trouble. He'd obviously given her one of those counseling things they do. And I'll tell you something else, that Caleb guy was definitely pals with Nila. They were as thick as thieves." The two residents nodded in mutual agreement.

Lexi and Scott shared a look.

"Is he the one you're investigating?" Patrick asked after a moment.

Lexi nodded once and turned to him. "Then what?"

He sighed. "When we woke up the next morning, Maisie was

gone. I thought someone would probably come and wipe our memories, but no one turned up."

Their quiet conversation was interrupted by a lady seated at a nearby table. "Phyllis, I think you've had the hot patootie for long enough, dear. It's time to share."

The other ladies at the table followed the comment with a burst of giggles.

The two young people looked up to see three of them staring adoringly at Scott.

He straightened and grinned. "There's more than enough of me to go around, ladies."

Lexi resumed eating her breakfast.

Patrick shook his head as he looked at the woman who'd called out. "Honestly, you'd think *she* was the dog."

Phyllis looked offended. "Patrick!"

"It was only a joke." He gave her a crooked smile and she tutted.

She wiped her mouth with her napkin. "I'm going for my morning walk."

"Don't forget your frame." He pointed to the walker near the table. "You don't want to get halfway round and have to be rescued again."

The woman gave him a withering stare and struggled to her feet.

Scott was out of his seat and around the table in two seconds to help her to the frame. "Perhaps while I'm here, I could give you physio. I'll catch up with you when we're settled."

Phyllis smiled and patted his arm. "I've had physio, but there's not much hope for these old bones."

"But you haven't had *my* physio." He waved his fingers in a pseudo-magical gesture.

She raised an eyebrow. "I might take you up on that if you can get your muzzle off. Our regular physio, who we've just been told has quit, is a lovely girl but she relied on concoctions which are of no use at all and they stank to high heaven."

Once she'd left, they finished their food and Stuart returned to give them the tour.

As they walked through a hallway to a large sitting room, Scott dangled his bracelet in front of their guide. "Why do I have to wear this? I'm not a resident."

The man looked awkward. "Sorry. It's the rule for all supes who aren't staff members."

They continued through the building while he pointed out fire exits and other safety features. Their tour finally took them into the basement and they paused at the bottom of the stairs. They were in a brightly lit hallway and a painting of a serious-looking man faced them on the wall.

"This is Jonas Maybury. He was the original owner of Emmersley."

"Ahh! The New England Mayburys." Lexi smiled when she was reminded of Betsy.

He pointed to the left. "Mr. Pick's room is along that hallway, room S-Eight. That's sub-level Eight."

They followed him to the right and into a gymnasium with weights and treadmills that didn't look like they saw much use.

Stuart picked a weight up. "You can use the facilities. It's a perk of staying here."

Scott wandered around the room and stopped at a set of doors. He opened them to reveal a darkened room. "What's this?"

The clerk hurried to him. "We're not allowed in there. Health and Safety rules. It used to be the hydrotherapy room, but they didn't have the money to finish the repairs to the tiles in the swimming pool."

Lexi imagined her friend's disappointment at finding a pool he couldn't use, but when he turned, she was surprised to see a look of satisfaction on his face.

He's planning something.

They glanced into the changing rooms at the end of a small hallway. On the way back, Stuart opened an office door and entered. He sorted through a pile of mail he'd carried.

She noticed a list of names on a whiteboard. It indicated that all residents received at least ten minutes of exercise twice a week. Most of them were simply encouraged to move around a little, walk a short distance, or lift a very small weight. It didn't seem very engaging. Studying the chart on the whiteboard, she noted that several names had been wiped away but they had been written there for so long, the board was lightly stained with the names David, Florence, Martin, and Maisie.

The clerk dropped the mail into the tray.

Lexi stepped out of the way to allow him to step out. "Whose office is this?"

He shrugged. "We used to have our own training staff but now, someone comes from an agency once a week. Or did. Kindred canceled that too."

Scott leaned against the wall. "What will you do about your physio leaving?"

Stuart stopped beside him. "I don't know if there's anything we can do. Previously, when Erika went on holiday, we'd get an agency replacement. I'd bet Kindred will want to send their person."

The sorcerer shrugged. "I'd be happy to offer my services while I'm here. If you're interested, that is. If you're not, that's fine too."

"Would your boss be okay about that?"

"What I do while he's asleep all day is up to me. I'm not asking for a job, merely offering to help."

Lexi could see the opportunity interested Stuart. "Do you mean regular physio or enhanced?"

"I could do either," Scott said casually, "but obviously, the magic helps."

The clerk thought for a moment, then looked around before

he spoke quietly. 'If you want to do that, it's best if you don't offer."

Scott frowned. "I don't understand."

"I'll make sure Nila sees your credentials. She always wants something for nothing. But if she thinks you want to do it, she'll happily say no and cut off her nose to spite her face."

He shook his head. "Good grief."

"Yeah, welcome to Emmersley." Stuart turned to Lexi. "And if you're qualified at anything, she'll probably try to get some work out of you too."

This wasn't good news for her as she needed to be free to look for Alicia and Bryan. "If I was qualified at something, do you think I'd work as a vampire's mobile buffet?"

The man looked awkwardly at his mail. "I need to finish dropping the rest of this."

He turned to Scott as they followed him through a hallway. "Nila told the residents that she would cover physio for now. I don't expect many would go. They'd rather suffer. If it gets out that you're qualified—" They turned the corner to find all six chairs outside the physio office were taken by ladies.

Lexi smirked. "I think the word is out."

Stuart held a hand up. "Ladies, I'm sorry, but Shaun is only visiting."

The women looked crushed.

Scott grinned. "I don't mind seeing what I can do for now."

The clerk thought about it and turned to the ladies. "Okay, but only this once. Do not breathe a word of this."

He headed upstairs and Lexi made her way to the gym. She looked into the hydrotherapy room but couldn't understand what her friend had seen to put that expression on his face. When she returned to the trainer's office, she looked around the desk, found the key to the filing cabinet in a drawer, opened it, and flipped through the resident files.

She found the file on David. It had *deceased* stamped on the front. "Hmm… No Florence, Maisie, or Martin."

A knock at the door made her jump.

"It's only us." Dick entered and waved Marcel's paw. He walked to the desk and sat opposite her. "We need to get this done and get out of here."

"What's wrong?"

"I'm bored. And look at poor Marcel. He's so sad."

She looked at the puppy, who didn't look sad in the slightest. "I'll take him for a walk shortly. Make sure you don't get caught out here. You're supposed to be asleep." Lexi closed and locked the drawers and stepped out of the room.

The vampire wandered off and she found a back staircase and made her way to the second floor. She crept along the quiet hallway and looked at each door. Most had nameplates but a few didn't. She tried the handle of one with no name assigned. It swung open to reveal a bedroom with a bare mattress and an empty closet. She stepped out, closed the door, and continued her exploration. A little farther along, she passed Phyllis's room and paused at an open doorway. Loud sounds emanated from within where a woman was seated in the chair next to her bed watching tv. Lexi shrugged and continued unnoticed.

The next door had no name—only an X on the nameplate and nothing more. Was it empty or not? Something about the door drew her to it, a warmth that somehow called to her.

Could it be Alicia? Some kind of twin connection?

Her heart thudded as she stepped closer and raised her hand toward the handle.

"What do you think you're doing?" Nila's acerbic voice grated the back of Lexi's neck.

She didn't react although inside, she thought she would have a heart attack. Instead, she turned slowly. "Hi. I'm looking for an empty room."

"You're Lena, Richard's…nail technician." The woman spoke the words like she was saying "blood whore."

"Yes, that's me." She abandoned the door reluctantly, approached Nila, and proffered her hand.

The woman glanced at her hand, then looked at her face. "Why are you looking for an empty room? Is the room you've been provided insufficient?"

"Oh, it's very nice." Lexi lowered her hand, relieved that she wouldn't have to touch the greasy woman. She enthused over the pokey little room on the top floor. "It's a lovely room, but there's no tv up there. The residents are already watching a quiz show downstairs and I usually watch something at this time. I thought an empty room would have an unused tv."

Nila looked at her with her pinprick eyes. "What do you like to watch?"

"I love those vacation home shows. I'm addicted." Lexi grinned as disarmingly as she could.

The woman stared at her like she thought it would make her break.

"The X means 'do not enter.' The previous inhabitant had a bad infection and the room has to be disinfected." She continued to stare, her expression grim and cold.

Lexi made a point of stepping away from the door and glanced at it with a grimace.

Finally, Nila said, "Follow me."

She walked along the hallway behind her unwanted guide and wondered if she might, with her reduced strength, be capable of snapping the horrible woman's neck and hiding her body in a closet. Regrettably, she discarded the idea. It did occur to her that she hadn't recognized her, so she clearly hadn't seen Alicia.

Nila stopped at an open door—the one with the woman inside watching tv. She walked in without knocking and Lexi followed.

"Anne?"

The little lady looked up and seemed positively terrified.

"This is Lena. She also likes those shows you love to watch. Would you mind if she joins you?" To Lexi, she said, "This is Anne Lown."

Anne looked at the girl and smiled. "You're late." She moved onto her bed and gestured to the chair she'd vacated. Lexi sat without a word.

Nila rolled her eyes. "Yes, of course. You would have expected her, wouldn't you?" Her tone was rude and sarcastic, which seemed to indicate that this career probably wasn't a vocation. She turned to Lexi. "Anne's a seer. Or she was when she still had all her marbles. I'll leave you to it." She gave her a smug smile and left.

Her jaw dropped. *What a way to talk about someone right in front of them.*

She turned to Anne, who looked hopefully at her and held a photo album out.

Where in the hell did that spring from?

The woman pointed at a photograph. "This is Leo. He was killed in the war."

Kill me now.

CHAPTER FIFTEEN

When she could finally make her escape, Lexi wandered past the gym to the physio room. No more ladies were seated outside but a woman left the treatment room and wandered past her. "He has magic hands, for sure." She giggled.

She knocked on the door frame.

Scott was writing notes. "Hey! Where were you at lunchtime?"

Lexi entered the room and looked around the anatomy charts on the walls. "Not eating. I'm starving. Are you ready?"

They headed to the dining room, ordered Chilli Con Carne, and went to sit with Patrick and Phyllis.

She kept her voice pitched low when she voiced her question. "What do you know about the resident in the room with an X on the nameplate."

Phyllis shook her head. "There's no one in there. Apparently, they're disinfecting the room, but it's been like that for a couple of weeks."

"Have you seen it empty?"

The woman seemed to think for a moment. "Not personally. Nila told us to steer clear of it because they were doing a deep clean. I thought it was strange because there hasn't been anyone in that room since Hilary passed, and that was a good two months before Nila arrived."

Lexi waited until someone had walked past the table before she continued. "Have you seen anyone go in or come out?

They both shook their heads and Patrick added. "But I don't frequent the ladies' level."

Scott leaned in with a conspiratorial eyebrow wiggle. "How do you feel about distracting the staff while we take a look in there tonight."

The man's eyes lit up. "An operation? Sure. But you won't need to do much distracting. We have a nurse in the on-call room and she'll be asleep. Then there are only the night boys. They are satyrs so as soon as Nila leaves, they'll wander off to drink and smoke dope in the greenhouse."

Phyllis and Patrick's food came out and the woman smacked her lips. "I love dinner. It's my favorite meal."

Her friend laughed. "What about breakfast?"

She looked at him. "Why, I love breakfast, Patrick. It's my favorite meal."

Lexi smiled. This was obviously a little mealtime ritual they had. She thought it was cute.

Phyllis glanced away and the smile slid from her face as her gaze froze on something behind Lexi. She knew instantly who it was. More than ever, she missed her enhanced perception and hated that someone nasty like Nila could creep up behind her.

"Mr. Green." It *was* Nila. "I know you think you're here for a holiday but your employer and I both think your time would be better spent contributing to our community. I understand you're a qualified physiotherapist. There's an office you can work from in the basement near the gym. Stuart will remove your inhibitor bracelet and show you to the office bright and early tomorrow morning. Let's see if we can't keep you busy."

Scott frowned. He put his fork on his plate as though the food had soured in his mouth. With an admirable show of resignation, he sighed.

Lexi was relieved to note that Nila didn't seem aware he'd already started work in that office.

"Miss Hearne."

Nuts.

"Anne enjoyed the time you spent with her today. Richard and I would like you to devote your days to providing companionship to the residents."

Richard and I. She made a mental eye-roll.

The two young people both looked at Nila, who smiled. "That should keep you both busy. I have a meeting to attend."

Patrick stared hard at the door swinging closed behind the woman. "Look at her sweeping out like a tour de France."

Scott frowned. "Don't you mean tour de force?"

The old man grinned. "No, I mean she's an old bike." He laughed.

Dinner plates were placed in front of Lexi and Scott.

She looked at the food. "I think I've lost my appetite."

Her friend was already on his third mouthful. He swallowed and looked sideways at her. "Are you kidding? You've been told to visit all the residents. I'd take that as permission to see them in their rooms—and anywhere else you feel like poking your nose."

"I never thought of that." She smiled.

Scott filled his next forkful of food. "You should probably wait a couple of hours until they're in their rooms and go make as many new friends as possible."

Her smile widened into a cheeky grin. "This might work out. Can you do a house call? Apparently, Anne Lown doesn't get out of her room very often."

He nodded. "And is Anne's room by any chance near room X?"

Lexi wiggled her eyebrows. "Maybe."

"As Nila's about to be out of the way at her meeting, I'll find

Stuart and see if I can get this band removed tonight. I'll stop by after." He waved his arm with the bracelet on it.

She hurried to Anne's room. The door was slightly ajar and as she approached, a loud shout came from within. It was Anne. "No, don't do it, please."

Instinctively, she slid a thin blade from the lining of her jacket, burst through the door, and went in low in case someone with a weapon might fire high. In a second, with the tip of the blade between her fingers ready to throw, she identified that no one other than Anne was in the room.

The woman looked at her where she crouched at her feet. "Hello, dear." She returned her eyes to the tv screen. "No, don't say yes to the dress. What's wrong with you? Turn and look at that back fat."

Lexi flopped onto the floor and groaned. She looked at Anne. "I feel like you did that on purpose."

"How would I possibly have known you were coming?" The resident's eyes glittered with mirth.

She scrambled to her feet and brushed herself down. "Hmph! I have my eye on you, madam." She cocked a half-grin. "Anne, I hope you don't mind but I've asked Shaun to come up and see you. He's a physio and I'd like to see if he can help you to move a little better."

Anne chuckled. "I don't think much will get these old bones moving again."

"Well, you never know. If you can get mobile, we can take you out of this room and go for a little walk."

"I'm happy to help if I can." The woman winked at her.

Lexi smiled. "We're the ones trying to help you."

Anne patted her hand. "Yes, dear."

Scott came around the corner and knocked on the door. "May I come in, ladies?"

"Oh, yes, of course." Anne looked at two young people. "What a beautiful couple you make."

"We're not a couple," Lexi quickly said. "We're only colleagues."

Again, the woman winked. "That's fine. Your secret is safe with me. But you can't fool a seer with matters of the heart."

Lexi looked at Scott's wrist. He no longer wore the bracelet. "I see Stuart obliged. How did he do it? Do satyrs have magic?"

He grinned with relief. "Not personally. He had a tuning fork and tapped the bracelet with it. It simply sprang open. Interesting little spell."

She chuckled. "You're such a spell nerd. I'll leave you to it, then." She hurried out.

As she closed the door, Scott said, "Good evening, Anne. My name's Shaun."

"If you say so, dear," Anne replied enigmatically.

Lexi hurried along the hall, intending to merely knock on as many doors as possible to get a look at the inhabitants. Twenty minutes later, she returned having only done two rooms. The residents both wanted company and she hadn't had the heart to leave them. She found Scott and Anne going through the photo album.

The resident pointed at the first photograph she'd shown Lexi earlier that day. "This is Wilfred. He died in the war."

"Leo," she corrected automatically.

"Pardon, dear?"

She pointed at the man in the picture. "You told me his name was Leo."

"Did I? Maybe it was." Anne flipped the book closed. "I don't know. It's not my album."

Her jaw dropped. "But what about all those pictures of you as a little girl?"

"I meant those pictures are representative of what I would have looked like as a young girl." The woman giggled when she shook her head.

Scott laughed. "You're a sneaky one."

Anne grimaced. "I'm sorry dears. I like the company and I don't get very much beyond the television."

A bark sounded from the hallway and the woman's eyes widened. "Did I hear a doggie?"

Marcel ran into the room, trailing his lead behind him.

A minute later, Dick arrived to find him on Anne's bed getting a tummy rub. "I'm so sorry. He ran off and this damn thing interfered with my speed." He waved his bracelet at them.

Lexi stared wide-eyed at him. "What are you doing up here at this time? Has anyone seen you?"

"I came up the back stairs. It's fine. No one saw me. Except for this lady, obviously."

Anne looked at him and blushed. "Oh, my! Well, this is embarrassing—to have all three of you here at once. I don't want any fights to break out here."

She looked at the two men and focused on Anne. "Why would we fight?"

"I saw the two of you kissing." The woman swiveled her pointing finger from Lexi to Dick.

The vampire shuddered.

Lexi shook her head quickly. "Yeah, no. That's not something that'll ever happen."

Anne put her hand to her cheek. "Oh, it hasn't happened yet? Oh, dear. I'm sorry. I do hate to give spoilers."

He smoothed an eyebrow. "Have they, by any chance, been giving you psychedelic drugs?"

"Oh, dear." she frowned. "Everything gets so mixed up these days. Well, out you all go. I'm tired and you have a busy night ahead of you." She passed Marcel to Lexi while Scott tucked her in.

The elderly lady smiled at him. "I feel so much better now. Thank you, dear. I think I might be well enough to take breakfast downstairs tomorrow."

He nodded. "That's great news. Good night, Anne."

"Good night, dear." She looked at Lexi. "I'm sorry she wasn't the right one."

She frowned in confusion. "What?"

Anne waved a hand nonchalantly. "Oh, that's only my silly brain again. Good night."

"So, has Nila definitely left for the evening?" she asked as she closed the door.

Dick glanced at his watch. "It's gone seven pm so I certainly hope so. Raj told me she's usually gone by six. The only reason she was there so late last night was because Patrick and his friends had gone AWOL."

Lexi nodded. "So how will we get Josh, Raj, and Stuart out of the way?"

The vampire grinned. "Patrick's already sent them looking for Marcel in the grounds after he ran off." He scratched the puppy behind the ears. "Didn't you, you naughty boy?"

She chuckled. "How long do you think they'll look for him?"

"Oh, they've already given up. According to Phyllis, they're in the greenhouse drinking and smoking pot."

Scott frowned. "Such dedication."

"As long as they're out of the way, I don't care what they're doing," she responded.

"I need to head to my room. I'll listen out and message you if it sounds like they're coming back into the building." Dick took a last speculative look at her and shuddered again.

She turned to her friend. "Can you take them downstairs? I don't want to risk them being seen."

He patted Marcel. "Sure. I'll be back in a second." He vanished with Dick and the puppy and reappeared alone.

The two of them walked in the direction of room X. They stood outside and checked the hallway once more before she tried the door. It was locked.

Scott muttered a word that was quickly followed by a satisfying click. "It's good to have that bracelet off."

Lexi opened the door. A dark lump on the bed confirmed the room was occupied. She breathed in and grimaced. "Good grief! What's that smell?" A woman lay handcuffed to the bed. Her head was turned away and her face was covered by her hair, the same color as hers.

"Alicia? Is that you?" She stepped in. Immediately, she felt dizzy and leaned against the wall. Her eyes were drawn to a strange yellow glow that issued from something on the dresser.

Scott stepped beside her. "Are you okay?"

She blinked and nodded. It was true. She *was* okay and felt better than she had in a long time, but she shook off the introspection. Still, she couldn't allow herself to become distracted by that or the horrible smell. She moved quickly to the bed.

"Alicia? It's okay. We're here to help you." She began to undo one of the wrist straps. Her fingers slipped in something greasy as she struggled with it.

Scott muttered. "You should make sure it's—"

With a wrist free, the woman whipped her arm and shoved her aside.

Lexi met the wall, slid to the floor, and tried to find her feet. The woman had the second strap untied in a moment and rose in a single unnatural movement to stand on the bed. She turned her face toward Lexi, who instantly saw the mistake she had made.

With her hair no longer swept across her face, it was obvious the woman wasn't her sister. She wasn't even certain it was a woman. There were no eyes, for one thing. The top half of the face was a blank canvas. A snout was positioned in the center and below that, a circular hole for a mouth with numerous tiny pointed teeth. Whatever it was turned its face to the source of the yellow light and threw itself toward it with its arms outstretched to snatch it.

Fortunately, it hadn't registered that its feet were still strapped to the bed. The creature landed face-first on the floor with its feet bound by the straps on the bed. While it had fallen several feet short of its goal, it had caught Scott by one foot and dragged him to the ground. It tried to get hold of him but the stinking, greasy substance frustrated its attempts.

Lexi panicked and forgot she was a mere human. She took one step closer and whipped her arm in the direction of the bed as she screamed, "Get back."

The creature arced onto its back on the bed. Scott looked at her in shock and she didn't have to ask. Her eyes were black again.

The creature appeared pinned to the bed by her command. She ignored her companion's stares and strapped one wrist, then walked around the bed with the intention to strap the other one. The closer she moved to the glowing object, the stronger she felt. Her head spun with the force of it. Excruciating pain flooded her arm and she looked at her scar. It had reappeared and was filled with a black substance as it had been in Lorenzo's apartment. She focused on the job at hand, continued around the bed, strapped up the creature's remaining wrist, and marched past Scott. In her hurry, she almost tripped over a black box on the floor with magical symbols drawn on it.

The sorcerer looked at it and frowned. "Should we—"

"Let's get out of here." Lexi was so freaked out by the demon, she only wanted to get out of the room.

He closed the door, locked it, and followed her to their rooms on the top floor.

Ten minutes later, she left the bathroom, having washed away the grease and changed her clothes. She stood at the wall mirror in her little room and stared at her eyes. They had returned to normal.

Scott knocked. "Can I come in?"

"Yes."

He looked uncertain as he studied her.

"What am I?" Lexi dropped onto her bed.

"You're still you." He sat beside her. "That's all that matters."

She was shaking. "I was so sure it would be her. What the hell was that?"

"A demon of some kind." He examined his leg where it had grabbed him. "Not a particularly high-level one, fortunately."

"Maybe there's some kind of monster inside me. Perhaps Delphine."

Scott sighed.

Dick appeared in the doorway. "Are you all right?"

Lexi rolled her eyes and looked at the sorcerer. "Did you call him up here?" She switched her gaze to Dick. "You still shouldn't be awake yet."

Instead of responding to her, the vampire looked at Scott. "I think you need to tell her."

She glanced from one to the other. "Tell me what?"

Her friend stared hard at Dick before he returned his gaze to her. "It's only a theory and not one that makes much sense at the moment." He paused but she remained focused on him and with a reluctant sigh, he continued, "You remember I said I'd read about people with black eyes?"

Lexi nodded.

"I found it again in a book about sorcerers. Specifically, dark sorcerers."

She wrinkled her brow in confusion. "There haven't been dark sorcerers for hundreds of years. I thought they all died out."

Dick leaned against the wall and folded his arms. "You and everyone else."

"Okay, so you said this doesn't make sense." She rubbed her forehead and scowled. "Do you mean because there *are* no dark sorcerers?"

Scott shifted a little uncomfortably beside her. "Well, that's certainly a factor but one I think I can explain. No, the problem lies in the magical source. You know that magical beings get their magic from different sources?"

Lexi nodded. "Yes, you source magic from the air and so does Dolores, and witches take theirs from the earth."

"Do you know where voodoo practitioners source theirs from?" he asked,

She sat for a moment in thought before she shook her head slowly. "Not a clue."

"They get their magic from the ancestor realms."

"So that's where dark sorcerers get theirs? The ancestor realms? It seems a tall order for me given that I don't know who my ancestors were."

He shook his head. "No, I'm merely introducing the concept of sourcing magic from other realms."

Lexi began to wonder if she would have to drag it out of him. "So, let's cut to the chase. I assume dark sorcerers would have taken their magic from the same place as dark fae."

"And you'd be wrong," Dick interjected.

Lexi stared at him. She wished her eyes hadn't returned to normal and—for now, at least—she was disappointed about that. In that moment, she'd have liked to scare the crap out of him. She looked at the scar, which remained half-filled with the black energy. Strangely, it gave her comfort.

Scott smirked. "He only knows that because he guessed wrong too."

She narrowed her eyes. "So you two have had conversations about this."

"Well—" Scott started.

"Yes," Dick finished.

Any number of smart retorts occurred to her, but she put her irritation aside. "So where *did* dark sorcerers draw their magic from?"

He drew a breath and held it for a moment before he answered. "From the demon realms."

Lexi thought about it. "We went through a portal that traversed a demon realm when we saved Dick from being cubed with a silver net. Could something have...latched on to me?" She shuddered.

"No. We'd have known. I think this has always been part of you but it was masked by your other legacy abilities."

She nodded slowly as the theory began to make sense to her. "And now, Alicia's got all the legacy abilities and because I used all your magic, this has somehow been activated?"

Scott nodded. "I think it's shown itself in tiny ways we haven't noticed. And Alicia doesn't have all the legacy abilities. I think that for the first time, she has hers and you have yours. In fact, it's likely that some of the dark sorcerer blood had been locked inside her until the two of you met."

Her analytical mind began to sift for holes in Scott's theory. "But no dark sorcerers were present when they first came together to make the legacies."

He gave her a crooked smile. "There may have been one."

Lexi could see exactly where he was going. "You're referring to that ridiculous myth about the one sorcerer who added his blood to the spell, aren't you?"

"It would explain this."

"I feel like you're making huge assumptions simply to fit your hypothesis. Anyway, this is all academic. I haven't been near any demon realms since Palm Springs. There wasn't one in New Orleans, or at the condo—oh!" She froze and remembered she hadn't told him about what had happened. She sighed. It was time to come clean. "This isn't the first time this has happened since New Orleans."

"The other night in Vegas?" he asked. "It's okay. Dick told me."

She stuck her tongue out at the vampire. "Traitor." She paused for a moment, then continued. "Something happened last night, too. I had a dream. I don't really remember it but when I woke up, I found a burn mark in the shape of my hand on the sheet."

"Why didn't you tell me?"

"It freaked me out. I didn't want to freak you out too. We have a job to do here."

"It's possible you might have come into contact with an object or substance that was somehow connected to the demon realms," Scott continued, although he frowned at her as though a little disappointed that she'd excluded him. "In New Orleans, that would have been Delphine's ring."

Lexi held a finger up. "But that magic was voodoo—ancestor realms. I have been listening, you know."

Dick picked an invisible thread from his jacket. "Do you remember I smelled sulfur at the scene of Jamal's murder? He was an amateur so he might have used something he shouldn't have in that ritual."

The sorcerer moved to the corner of her bed. "But that's where my theory stumbles. There doesn't seem to have been a demonic source in the condo or, as far as we can tell, in room X with the demon."

The vampire's eyes widened. "Are you kidding me? There was a demon in that room? Is that what the stink is? It's revolting. I tried not to say anything, though."

Scott stared at him. "You could have tried harder. Anyway. That smell is tallow, which is animal fat. The demon was covered in it."

Dick raised an eyebrow. "I wonder if it's anyone I know."

Lexi stared at him, then shook her head when he shrugged in response.

The younger man gestured impatiently. "It didn't appear to be up to your standard of conversation."

She found a towel and wiped her hands again, only too aware of the smell. "Couldn't the demon itself have connected me to the demon realms?"

He shook his head. "A demon that's stranded on this plane is about as connected to its realm as we are. I don't think it can act as a conduit to the demon realm. It can have its own power and lend it like Azatoth seems to do with Caleb. Anyway, I can't think of anything that you would have been able to draw on in Dick's condo."

"What about the eerie yellow light?" She put the towel aside. "What was that?"

Scott looked at Dick and then at her. "What yellow light? Where?"

"Coming from something on the dresser. It illuminated that demon's bedroom. You can't have missed it."

"The demon's bedroom was dark until I turned the light on. I didn't see any yellow light."

Lexi turned to the vampire. "Jesús wore a pendant that glowed with that same strange yellow light that night at the condo."

Dick's brow wrinkled as he pinched his lower lip in thought. "Pendant? A little glass tube?"

She nodded quickly. "Yes, I think it was a tube."

He stroked his chin absently. "Interesting. That's brimstone. He's a superstitious little soul and says it protects him from evil spirits."

The reality of the discussion struck her. She sighed. "So, just like that, I'm an evil sorcerer now."

"Do you feel evil?" Dick asked.

Lexi sighed. "I don't know what I feel."

Scott stood. "The glowing object was on the dresser?"

She nodded and he vanished.

He reappeared moments later. "We have a problem."

CHAPTER SIXTEEN

Lexi, Scott, and Dick appeared in the small, windowless bedroom.

"We really should do that more often. It's so expedient." The vampire looked around and shuddered. "Eugh! That stench."

She stared at the bed, which was unoccupied. "Oh!" Her gaze slid immediately to the strange little box to find it was now open and also empty. She wondered what had been in it.

Scott examined one of the greasy straps. It didn't look broken and he focused his gaze on her. "How tightly did you redo the straps?"

Her face flushed. "I didn't want to hurt it."

Dick raised an eyebrow. "Yes. You are clearly an evil sorcerer. Exhibiting that much empathy was a totally evil sorcerer thing to do."

A squeal made them jump and Lexi raced to the other side of the bed. The demon crouched, grasped a small creature with bat-like ears in its fist, and held it against the wall. The little thing was almost crushed and beat its tiny arm against its captor's hand.

The demon seemed to try to squeeze through a small hole in

the wall. It had managed to get its head through, but the aperture wasn't big enough for the rest of it to follow. Its captive squealed again. She had no idea what it was, but it was clearly suffering.

Scott inspected the barrier. "Look how the wall's wavering around this little monster. I think the demon's somehow using it to create a portal."

Dick squinted at it. "Could it be a thinner?"

Lexi retrieved a shuriken and threw it at the demon's hand, which sprang open and allowed the little creature to scuttle away.

The moment the demon lost contact, the hole in the wall disappeared. Unfortunately for the demon, its head was already on the other side of it. It's body, from the neck down, fell clumsily.

The vampire grimaced. "Oops."

When she looked at the dresser, the object was gone but a slight glow came from the wall where the portal had been. She could make out a rough yellow circle, not much bigger than the demon's head, drawn on the surface. Curious, she crouched to where the little creature attempted to hide under the bed while its hand softly glowed in the dark. "What's a thinner?"

"I've heard of them," Scott answered. "It's a kind of demon that can be used to make the veil between dimensions—"

"Thinner," she finished. "So this is one?"

He looked at Dick and the vampire crouched to look under the bed. He straightened after a moment. "I don't know, honestly. I've never seen one. But if I had to make an educated guess…"

It crept toward her. Instinctively, she skittered away from the wall until her head hit the side of the dresser. "Ow! Shit."

The small, black, scaled creature had huge, amber eyes and its wide bat-like ears twitched. It held itself in apparent pain and whimpered before it flopped onto the floor.

Lexi moved closer to it. "I wonder how it got here." She was aware of Scott shuffling closer. "Be careful. Don't touch it. For all we know, it could be poisonous."

Slowly, she extended her hand to the being, which shrank away from her as best it could and made a frightened, trilling sound. "Hey, little guy, it's okay. I'm only going to try to help you."

"*Little guy?*" Dick whispered. "Even if it's not a thinner, it is some kind of demon. It'll probably elongate its jaw and bite your arm off. I can't watch."

She flicked a glance at him and smirked when she saw he watched from between his fingers. When she looked at Scott, he'd pulled his face back so far he'd given himself a double-chin. She rolled her eyes at the two of them. When her hand was close enough that she'd still be able to pull it away quickly, she held it still and simply waited to see what the demon would do. It moved forward tentatively and sniffed her. The pupils in its giant eyes became huge, and its arm reached toward her almost in slow motion before it grasped her hand with long spindly fingers.

Two sharply drawn breaths behind her made her smile.

The moment they touched, the glow from the creature's hand brightened and she felt her unhealing scar tickle. It scampered up her arm and hugged against her shoulder.

Dick covered his eyes. "Dear God, it'll bite her head off."

A quick glance confirmed that he had covered his eyes with his hands. "Hey, Prince of Darkness. Look, it's fine." She shook her head, completely at a loss to explain why she trusted it.

She could see that while the hole was gone, the wall still appeared to be in a state of flux. "Hey, little guy, do you need the portal to get home?" She lifted the creature away from her shoulder and held it closer to the wall. "You should be able to get back to wherever you came from now."

He tightened his hold on her hand and refused to let go.

Lexi turned to her companions. "Should I shove it through?"

It squawked and raced up her arm again.

The sorcerer sighed. "I think this little…uh, whatever it is—"

"Demon, Scott," Dick supplied. "It's a demon."

He shrugged. "Okay, this little demon doesn't seem to want to go in there. Maybe all the big demons pick on it."

"No personification of the monster. I absolutely forbid it." The vampire stepped closer to Lexi and attempted to take the creature. "Fine, I'll take it outside and crush it with a rock." He leapt back and cradled his hand. "The little bastard bit me."

"Well, now you know what it's like." Scott smirked.

"I already know what it's like. How do you think I became a vampire? Osmosis?" Dick retreated. "I'll simply let the little fucker cling to you like a limpet, but if he tries to eat Marcel, all bets are off."

"Fine. What will we do about this?" Lexi pointed at the corpse.

Scott stooped and took an arm. "Let's get it on the bed, strap it, and leave it how we found it."

She moved to grab its feet. "It's a start."

Dick raised an eyebrow at her. "Someone will notice it doesn't have a head. It won't look good that you were seen snooping here and the next time someone checks, the demon has no head."

The two men took an arm each and they swung it onto the bed and retied the straps at its wrists and ankles.

The little creature scrambled off Lexi's shoulder and scampered to the wall.

The vampire glanced at it. "At least your little limpet's going back to wherever it came from. That's one less problem."

Scott looked at the headless corpse on the bed. "Maybe we could burn it."

He pinched the bridge of his nose. "Great idea. Let's leave a packet of cigarettes. Perhaps Nila will think it was smoking in bed."

Lexi rounded on him. "You're not being very constructive."

"Erm… Guys." Scott stared at the wall and they turned as one.

The little creature had pushed its arms through the undulating surface and now pulled at something. It tugged a few times, placed its little black feet on either side of the hole, and yanked harder. After a loud popping sound, it sprawled on the floor with two fingers up the nostrils of the demon's snout and one in its mouth like a bowling ball. It squealed, dropped the head, and studied a finger that had caught on one of the pointy teeth. Strange chattering noises followed as it kicked the head and rolled it to Lexi's feet. It climbed her leg, then her arm, and settled onto her shoulder.

Dick turned to Scott. "So, how exactly does this counseling work? Could I hire you to eradicate the last few minutes?"

She picked the head up by the hair and plopped it onto the corpse. "There, perfect." It immediately rolled across the pillow. Speculatively, she looked at the black energy running through her scar.

Why not?

Before she could change her mind, she put the head in position, slapped her hand over the scar, and pointed a finger at the demon. "Stay put."

The three of them stared as the head sealed itself to the neck. She was delighted. "I have my mojo back."

Dick shook his head. "That's definitely not the mojo you had before."

Ignoring him, she turned excitedly to Scott but he simply frowned. "What?"

"*Stay put?* Mutter it, at least. You'll give sorcerers a bad name."

Lexi pointed at the demon. "But look what I did."

The little black creature on Lexi's shoulder made an "Oooooooh!" sound.

The vampire raised an eyebrow. "You impressed the little demon."

She shrugged. "I'll take what I can get."

He leaned close to the corpse's neck. "God, this thing stinks. But I can't even see the join. You did a good job."

The demon's eyes snapped open and a high-pitched howl issued from its mouth.

Dick screamed and leapt back several feet.

Scott's jaw dropped.

Lexi stepped forward as it began to sit and punched it in the head, and it flopped unconscious.

The three of them stood and simply stared, not quite willing to believe the evidence of their own eyes.

She opened her mouth to say, "Let's get out of here," when a key rattled in the lock. Scott caught their hands and muttered softly. A moment later, they were in her room.

Scott frowned. "How the fuck did you do that? You reanimated it."

"I don't know what that means." She picked a towel up.

"You brought it back to life." He gestured wildly with his hands to punctuate his words.

Lexi shrugged as she wiped her arms. "I don't know how demons work. Its head is on and I thought that was what we wanted." She was being intentionally obtuse and was well aware of what had happened. It terrified her and excited her in equal parts. "I wonder who was going into the room."

He narrowed his eyes. "I'll take a quick look."

"Wait. Be careful and stay invisible."

The sorcerer rolled his eyes and vanished.

Dick stared at the little creature on her shoulder. "I can't believe you brought that with you. They'll know someone was in there when they see it's gone."

"Or when they see the demon's blood on the wall and floor from its temporary beheading." She shrugged and sat on her bed. They both remained silent for a minute.

The vampire looked at his watch. "What's keeping him? Should we go down?"

Scott reappeared. His eyes were wild, and he looked slightly green. He sat heavily on the chair.

Lexi was instantly alert. "What happened?"

He focused on her. "It was Nila."

"Did she notice something different?" She stood anxiously. "Did she see the blood on the wall?"

He exhaled a slightly panicked breath and raised his eyebrows. "I don't think the blood on the wall will be an issue. She killed it."

Dick narrowed his eyes. "Scott, you've seen demons killed before. You've done it yourself. What has you so freaked out."

Scott shook his head. "It was so…visceral. That box you almost tripped over on the floor—she held it over the demon asking, 'Where is it?' I'd guess that's where your little friend was. The demon only made that whining noise. Nila lost it and pounded the box into its face. Then, she threw it aside and ripped its head off with her bare hands."

The vampire folded his arms and leaned against the wall. "It lost its head again? I'm not a fan of demons but that one had a seriously shitty day. I feel sorry for it."

Lexi bit her lip. "What the hell is Nila doing?"

The sorcerer shuddered. "Nothing good. What now?"

Dick stood and his face brightened. "Go down and put its head on again."

After a moment, both Lexi and Scott asked, "Why?"

He smirked. "To screw with Nila. Can you imagine her face?"

Scott shook his head. "What happened to you feeling sorry for the demon?"

He picked an invisible thread from his shirt cuff. "It comes and goes."

They stopped speaking at the sound of approaching footsteps.

"Hellooo. Hello?" Patrick's voice came through the door as he knocked.

Lexi looked urgently at Dick. "He might not be alone."

Scott disappeared with Dick and returned alone a moment later.

She spoke loudly. "Hi, Patrick. Come in."

"I'm sorry to disturb you. I wanted to check you were all okaaaaaa— Holy Mother of God. What the fuck is that?"

In her rush to get the vampire out of the room, she had somehow forgotten the creature. She turned and looked into the saucer-like eyes of the little being clinging to her shoulder and peeking out from behind her. "It's my…cat."

An awkward silence settled on the room. She looked at the two men in turn and their faces indicated that they had come to the same conclusion.

No way does this look like a cat.

"Monkey," she finished. "It's my cat monkey."

Remarkably, a silent consensus was reached by everyone in the room, and each person seemed prepared to go with it.

"Does your…uh, cat monkey have a name?" Patrick seemed to struggle to get "cat monkey" out of his mouth.

Lexi turned and looked at her shoulder. She was almost touching noses with the creature and its giant eyes stared unblinkingly into hers. "Limpet. His name's Limpet." She smiled confidently at the old man.

"All right." He looked directly at the strange, black, hairless demon. "Hello, Limpet." He stepped forward and extended a hand. "Is he friendly?"

She stepped back while Scott blocked his path.

"He's nervous around new people," she explained hastily.

"Very nervous." The sorcerer nodded furiously.

Limpet had disappeared behind her and she could feel him clinging to her hair. "You wanted to know about the operation. I'm afraid it was a bust."

"I'm sorry to hear that. So, whoever was in there wasn't who you were expecting?"

Scott clapped him on the back. "*Absolutely* not who or what we were expecting."

"That's a shame. What's plan B?" Patrick looked around the room. "There is a plan B, isn't there?"

Lexi had convinced herself that she had been about to find her sister. She hadn't thought past that room. "They might be in another building on the property. We'll need to explore the grounds."

The resident looked disappointed.

Scott put his hand on the man's shoulder. "We'll let you know how it goes."

Patrick left the room, still looking a little despondent, and she reached to the demon. He jumped onto her hand and she held him close to her face. "Hello, Limpet."

He scrunched his giant eyes closed and when he opened them, they were a quarter of the size and looked exactly like a cat's eyes.

She gaped. "Do you see this?" She didn't bother to turn to Scott and instead, put Limpet onto the bed and watched.

The little creature began to shake. He vibrated so fast, he actually blurred. Suddenly, a shock of black fur erupted all over his body. His hands still had little fingers, though, and he stretched his arms toward her. She could see something in his hands. He opened them to reveal a ring with a yellow crystal. The stone glowed and reflected eerily in Limpet's little golden eyes.

Lexi stared at the ring and realized that this was the source of the light she had caught glimpses of in the demon's room. "I wondered what the glow was."

Scott frowned in confusion. "What glow?"

She looked from Scott to the ring and back again. "You don't see a yellow glow coming from this stone?"

"Nope."

Her head tilted curiously, she studied Limpet. "Is that for me?"

He pushed the ring closer to her face. When she took it, his hands changed into paws. He purred, curled comfortably, and closed his eyes.

Lexi held the ring and studied it. The yellow light it gave off was entrancing. She held it over her finger.

Scott took a step forward. "Erm…maybe you shouldn't—"

Before he could finish, she slipped it onto her finger. Immediately, a warm feeling radiated from her hand. Her scar tickled, then ached, and the black energy seemed to come to life with sparkling specks of yellow.

She closed her eyes and felt the magic rise within her.

Every nerve-ending in her body and every pore in her skin came to life. It felt wonderful and she groaned with pleasure. Her eyes were black. Somehow, she knew that and kept them closed.

"Erm… Lexi?" Scott sounded a little strangled like he couldn't quite breathe properly. "Maybe I should wait outside. You seem to be having a…moment."

The magic surged through her veins and settled in her core. She felt her bones harden and her muscles tighten. When the wave had settled over her, she knew her eyes had returned to normal. She opened them and stared ahead.

"Oh, boy," Scott whispered. "You are definitely a dark sorcerer. But your eyes aren't black. That has to be good, right?"

Lexi looked at him. "We have work to do."

He frowned. "Work?"

She stood and put her hands on her hips. "I'm all charged up with no place to go."

In response, he simply stared at her with a bemused expression on his face.

A little impatient, she poked his arm. "What was your first lesson in sorcery?"

Scott exhaled slowly as he tried to remember. "I learned to meditate for a year or so."

Her face scrunched in distaste before she raised an eyebrow. "Yeah, we're gonna go ahead and skip that part."

Limpet stretched, curled again, and went to sleep.

The sorcerer took her arm and they translocated.

CHAPTER SEVENTEEN

The friends appeared in the cover of trees and a safe distance from the building.

Lexi looked around. "Why didn't we do this at the house?"

Scott shook his head. "We don't know what we're dealing with here. It's best if you don't blow the residents up."

She nodded. "That makes sense. So, what will we do, Obi-Wan?"

He froze and stared at her. "Lexi Braxton. You referenced Star Wars. You've only been a sorcerer for five minutes and you're already cooler."

"Calm down, nerd." She rolled her eyes. "It'll never happen again."

His grin was a little smug and he looked around. "We need to see what else might be happening here on the property, so we may as well make the first lesson how to use spellglass balls. Don't be worried if this doesn't work. Hold your hand out and picture a small glass sphere with a mirrored finish, about the size of a golf ball. Its purpose is to hurtle around and gather information that you will look at when it returns. Basically, it's the mirror spell I use." He held his hand out and a little mirrored ball appeared in his palm.

Lexi repeated his motions. She closed her eyes, opened them again, and frowned. Her hand was empty. "Where is it supposed to come from?"

He sighed. "This is why we meditate. Some concepts simply can't be explained in words."

"We don't have time for this." She fiddled in the lining of her vest, retrieved a shiny silver bullet, and held it between her finger and thumb. "Will this do?"

Scott looked at it a little cautiously. "I guess, but make sure you don't blow your hand off."

She put it into her palm, closed her hand around it, and recalled him making her pendant. When she opened her hand, it was a sphere but it had turned dark like hematite.

"Why did it come out like that?" She frowned. "Is it because of the dark sorcery?"

"I don't think so. My guess is that maybe, deep down, you're afraid of what you are, and it affects what you're doing—"

"I wouldn't say it's deep down," she muttered. "I'm fairly terrified on the surface."

"There's no reason why you shouldn't have been able to create a silver ball," he continued. "Never mind, it should work fine. Next, you want to levitate it and send it in a circle above us."

His ball rose slowly into the sky while hers rocketed from her hand.

Scott looked at her. "It's not a race."

She shrugged. "Okay. But if it was, I'd have won." She closed her eyes. "Oh!"

"What's up?"

"This is so cool." She grinned. "I didn't think it would work like this. I can see what the ball sees."

"You can?" His voice sounded higher-pitched than usual.

Lexi opened her eyes. "Is that wrong?"

"No. It simply never occurred to me to do that." Scott closed his eyes but immediately frowned. "It doesn't work for me. Maybe it's in how you created it in the first place." He sounded slightly annoyed. "Okay, let's each take a half of the property. If you need to follow yours as it flies, I'll keep watch down here."

She closed her eyes again and focused as her ball moved to the edge of the property, through an orchard, around barns, and past several lodges. "Only one of the lodges looks lived in but it seems to be empty right now."

Her half of the property was covered in minutes so she sent the sphere to the other side and investigated a storage building and some beehives. Scott's floated along and she raced past it several times before she called hers back. "Well, there's no construction work going on here."

He shrugged. "We need to search the whole house from top to bottom. If we can't find your sister, maybe we could ask Dick to get information out of Nila tomorrow night. She seems quite fond of him, you know, when she's not ripping heads off."

Lexi smirked. "I somehow don't think the feeling's mutual. But you're right. He might at least be able to get her out of the way. Come on. It's almost time for him to be awake. You ask him about distracting Nila tomorrow night and I'll check on Limpet."

She entered the room to find the creature still asleep exactly where she'd left him. Intrigued, she watched him for a few moments while he slept. He looked exactly like a cat. When she attempted to stroke his ear, his giant, saucer-like eyes snapped open and he bolted off the opposite side of the bed. He struck the wall at speed. It wobbled and he vanished through it.

With a sigh, she straightened and stared at the wall. He'd gone and she couldn't help but feel a little disappointed. She turned to leave but heard a squeak behind her. When she turned, his face appeared from the wall. He gazed warily around the room before he pushed into it again. The little demon leapt onto the bed, screwed his eyes shut, and became a cat once more. He kneaded the covers and purred.

"I'm going for a walk. Do you want to come?" Lexi left the room and Limpet followed.

They headed toward the basement and she could hear an argument from halfway down the stairs.

"I absolutely and positively refuse." Dick was definitely upset about something.

"But we've looked almost everywhere," Scott replied.

She put her head around the door a little cautiously. Dick stood in front of Scott and they were nose to nose.

The vampire spoke as if through gritted teeth. "I don't care. I won't do it."

"I can hear you two halfway to the dining room. What's going on?" Lexi stepped into the room.

Dick turned to her. "I am as dedicated, professional, and loyal an employee as Dolores could ever hope for. I work ridiculous hours, I spend more on this job than I earn, and I'm even prepared to put up with you two lunatics. But this is simply too much."

She raised her palms in a placatory gesture. "Dick, calm down. What has Scott asked you to do?"

"He wants me to— Jesus, I can't even say the words." He put his palm to his forehead.

Lexi stood and waited while she wondered what Scott had said.

The vampire took a deep breath. "Scott has suggested I…take one for the team."

She almost laughed but instead, shook her head in apparent confusion. "Take one what?"

He put his hand on his chest. "He wants me to take Nila and— dear God, and *pump her*. I think I'll throw up."

"Oh, that." She smirked. "I asked him to ask you."

"Excuse me?"

"If we can't find out where Caleb has Ali and Bryan, I thought you could…" She winked and clicked her tongue a couple of times for effect. "You know, pillow talk and whatnot. She seems to have taken a shine to you."

"I'm calling Dolores." Dick took his cell phone out.

Lexi chuckled. "Put that away, for goodness sake. No one's asking for you to go that far. Scott was supposed to ask you to take her out for a drink tomorrow night and pump her for information so we can finish searching the place."

The vampire pointed accusingly at the other man. "That's not what he said."

She looked at Scott.

He grinned. "Sorry. You should have seen his face, though."

Dick wheeled to stare at him, his face red. "I'll feed you vampire blood, then kill you. And when you wake up, I'll keep breaking all your bones just for fun."

The sorcerer chuckled. "Would that make you my dad?"

"Fuck off." He stormed to the door and held it open. "Get out, the pair of you."

"What are you doing?" Lexi asked.

With a long-suffering sigh, he stopped in the doorway and turned. "Getting ready to invite Nila on a date. It'll take at least a day of meditation." He looked at Limpet. "Do you intend to keep that?"

She shrugged. "Sure, why not?"

He gaped at her. "You don't even know what it eats."

"I'll figure it out."

A *yip* drew their attention. She looked to where Limpet leaned into Marcel's food bowl.

"We might be about to find out now," Scott said.

The cat-demon picked a handful of dog food up, sniffed it, and fell on his butt as he rubbed his nose in disgust. Marcel approached cautiously and sat on his haunches with his head tilted to stare at the little creature.

Limpet, who still had a lump of dog food in his hand, held his arm out and the puppy licked it out of his hand. He giggled and Marcel yipped again and wagged his stumpy tail.

The demon took another lump of dog food and the process was repeated.

"Not dog food, apparently. You have another half-hour before you said you'd be awake. Come on, Limpet." Lexi walked out of Dick's room. Scott and Limpet followed.

She turned to her friend in the hallway. "What's next for you?"

He looked at the time. "I'm meeting Phyllis."

"Really? It's late for work."

"I wanted some quiet when I see her."

They headed through the gym toward the physio room. Limpet found a mirror and sat in front of it to study himself.

Phyllis waited outside the room.

Scott smiled. "Sorry to keep you waiting."

She leaned on her walker and stood. "I was early."

While he washed his hands, Lexi helped her step up to sit on the bed. Scott returned and looked at her bracelet. "This won't help." He muttered a spell and her bracelet jumped with a spark and stayed where it was.

"Ow!" She yanked her arm back.

"I need…" He looked around the little room, opened a glass-fronted cupboard, and pulled out a wide box. Without an explanation, he opened the box and selected a long piece of metal. He studied it for a moment, looked at Phyllis, and nodded.

The woman recoiled and stared at the long, curved, shiny piece of metal in his hand. "What is it?"

"It's a Graston tool. It's only a physio tool for rubbing over muscles."

Hesitantly, she held out her arm again and he tapped the metal against it. As it chimed, he muttered. Instead of fading, the tone went higher. When it reached the right note, the bracelet fell and the old woman rubbed her wrist and nodded her thanks.

"Oh!" She suddenly looked alarmed.

"What's wrong?" he asked.

Phyllis shook her head. "My senses came back. I can tell you're a sorcerer now. You smell of ozone."

He chuckled. "It's an occupational hazard."

She stared at Lexi. "I don't understand. I thought you were human."

"Let me guess—brimstone." She rolled her eyes. "We're still trying to confirm what I am."

The woman narrowed her eyes. "Really? You smell a little like a demon."

"I'll wait outside," she said with a sigh.

When she returned to the gym, Limpet remained motionless in front of the mirror. She spent a few minutes trying the weights, then decided to see how Dick was getting on. As she approached the hallway around the corner from his room, the sound of voices made her pause.

"I shouldn't make an exception but as you'll only be with us a short time and Marcel is so adorable, I've decided I'll let him stay. But your staff must be better behaved. I can't have them wandering around the building alone."

"I quite agree, Nila," he responded,

Lexi realized the voices were getting closer. She stood next to the painting of Jonas Maybury. A door stood on either side of the indented wall and she opened one. It was a cleaning closet and she stepped in quietly and closed the door.

She felt around in the dark and put her hand on what seemed to be a stick with a hard, cold handle. It was better than nothing, she decided and picked it up to hold it ready in case she was discovered.

Silently, she asked herself, *Am I prepared to bludgeon that woman to death if she opens this door?*

The answer was a resounding yes.

Moments later, the voices were directly outside the door.

"Well, I'm sure Lena will be along shortly," Dick said. "I'll speak to her." After a moment, he added a loud, high-pitched, "Oh! Erm. Righto."

Lexi heard him walk in the direction of his room and Nila take the stairs. She gave it a minute before she left and knocked on his door. She waited but he didn't respond.

After a few moments, she knocked again. "Dick?"

The door was yanked open and he pulled her in. "Thank God it's you."

"What's wrong?"

"That woman is disturbing. She was here a few minutes ago and walked in without even bothering to knock. I'd heard her shoes on the floor and wasn't ready to admit to being awake yet so I jumped into bed and pretended to be asleep. She simply stood there and stared at me for about five minutes. She didn't move a fraction of an inch. Then she—" Dick paused as though he didn't want to finish.

"She what?"

He shuddered. "She smelled me."

Lexi stared at him.

"She leaned right next to my face and sniffed. It was the creepiest thing that has ever happened to me in my life. Her breath was disgusting. And I felt so...exposed."

She guffawed. "Clearly, you've never been on the last Metro-Rail train. That shit happens all the time. You're standing there minding your own business when some creep starts sniffing your hair. I've ruptured so many balls that way." She smiled fondly at the memory, then blinked and looked at him. "Wait, if you were pretending to be asleep, how do you know she was staring at you?"

"What else is there to look at in here? And I felt her eyes on me." He shuddered again. "Finally, I had to fake waking up and she started to speak to me like everything was normal. I managed to start walking her along the hallway past where you were hiding in the closet at the bottom of the stairs. I thought *she* might hear your heart beating, never mind me."

"I almost walked into the two of you. I barely escaped."

"Speaking of escape, we need to get out of here. That woman looks like she won't leave me alone, and she won't keep her hands off my ass. I'm ready to report her to Human Resources."

Lexi shook her head and hid a grin. "There is no Human Resources department. They were all fired on Friday so Kindred can take their roles."

Dick sat in an armchair and pulled his shoes on. "Hardly surprising, I suppose."

"It's good for us. We have to find my sister and brother-in-law and the missing residents. When you two go out on your date, we'll search properly."

He sighed. "As she was still around, I asked her out for a drink tonight but she said no because she was heading out for a meeting with the new owner. It means Caleb's definitely around here somewhere. Here's hoping he can keep her interest for a couple of hours and we can get the job done. Then, I won't have to take her for a drink tomorrow night."

She thought for a minute. "Good. Let's go through this place from top to bottom."

Lexi returned to the physio room and waited for Scott to open the door.

Phyllis was seated and flexed this way and that. "I can't remember the last time I felt so good."

He moved to help her, but she hopped down herself. "I have another suggestion for you," he said. "Come with me."

The two left the physio room and walked past Lexi. She glanced at Phyllis's walker still in the room, smiled, and followed them to the big double-doors at the end of the gym.

The old woman looked at Scott with confusion on her face. "I think this used to be the swimming pool. They stopped using it before I arrived."

He opened the door and switched the light on as they entered. The room was empty except for a single chair and a few boxes of tiles. It looked like they'd given up halfway through the repairs. A long wooden plank went from the side into the three-foot shallow end of the empty pool. "I thought you might appreciate somewhere to work out the kinks. I think it could help with your arthritis."

A look of fright appeared on her face. "You want me to shift? I'm not sure."

Scott indicated their surroundings. "There's no one in here to hurt and I'm here if you need me. How about you sit here and think about it. See if it's something you'd like to do in a safe environment. I'll come back for you in around twenty minutes."

"I suppose I could think about it." The old woman walked to the chair and sat with her hands in her lap.

Lexi looked at her. She didn't think Phyllis would shift as she seemed so uncomfortable at the mere thought of it.

The two friends returned to the physio room and Scott sprayed sanitizer on the bed and wiped it.

He looked at the time. "Anne Lown is next."

She watched him work at this role that didn't involve hunting rogue supernaturals and thought it suited him. "I'll go upstairs and collect Anne" She turned. "Nila rejected Dick in favor of a date with Caleb tonight. We need to stay vigilant if he's around."

The sorcerer nodded.

As she hurried through the gym to the elevator, she glanced at where Limpet curled in sleep next to the mirror.

Anne was seated in a wheelchair beside her bed when she arrived. "You're right on time."

Lexi flicked the chair's brake off with her foot. "How are you feeling?"

The woman turned in the chair to stare at her. "I feel nervous. It's a big day."

She negotiated the doorway and pushed the chair toward the elevator. "It is? Is it your birthday?"

Anne laughed. "Not for me. It's a big day for you. No spoilers, though."

As she pushed the chair through the gym, she noticed that Limpet had moved off and wondered if she should have called him when she went up. She hoped he wasn't lost in the big house.

Lexi delivered Anne to Scott's office and closed the door behind her.

She returned to Dick's room.

"Is Limpet in here?"

The vampire looked at Marcel, who was snoozing alone on his bed. "No. We'll probably find him while we're searching the —" His face suddenly became alert. He turned to the door and tilted his head. "I thought Nila had left already. She's coming back." He looked wildly around the room and finally, his gaze landed on her. "Lexi, I'm truly sorry about this."

He put his arm around her waist and pulled her against him, clamped his other hand on the back of her neck, and kissed her.

Her first instinct was to knee him in the groin, but damn if Dick wasn't the best kisser by a mile that she'd ever experienced. She grasped his hips a second before the door opened.

"Disgusting!" Nila spun and marched away. Her heels echoed loudly along the hall.

The vampire released her. "You may rupture my balls now. If that woman leaves me alone, it was worth it."

Lexi stared incredulously at him. "You are really, *really* good at that."

He smoothed an eyebrow and preened. "Why, thank you. Years of training. Goodness, I haven't kissed a woman like that since Marilyn Monroe."

"Wait, you kissed Marilyn Monroe?"

Dick picked an invisible piece of fluff from his shirt. "Yes, for a dare."

"What was it like?"

"Painful." He rolled his eyes. "Her husband at the time, Joe DiMaggio, broke my nose. It was quite a scandal."

"Okay." She was impressed, there was no hiding it. After a moment, she looked around. "Where's Marcel?"

The vampire looked under the bed. "He must have gotten out when she opened the door."

CHAPTER EIGHTEEN

Nila pushed the bar on the fire exit and flung it open.

She stamped up the outside steps to ground level. Marcel struggled in her arm, but her hold tightened. She walked across the lawn to the copse of trees surrounding the house and shoved him into the branches of a tree. He slipped and regained his balance, looked doubtfully at the ground, then stared fearfully at her.

While she glowered at him, she took the silver whistle from around her neck and hung it in a branch of the same tree. She didn't move her gaze from his as she kicked her shoes off and began to change.

The puppy whined as spiky antlers pushed through her scalp and her nose and jaw elongated into a snout. Her shoulders broadened and her spine curved with immense cracking sounds. The clothes shredded as she transformed and she ripped them away with her hands as they turned into long, menacing claws. Nila growled and saliva slid through pointed teeth.

Marcel lost his balance and fell but was caught in the whistle's cord on the way down. He yelped as he landed and something cracked, and he tried to limp away.

He didn't manage more than a few feet, in pain and tangled in the whistle as he was. The woman had completed her change and stalked the injured puppy slowly, snorting and slavering.

Unable to walk on his injured hind leg, Marcel stumbled and fell. He scrambled a few more inches as her gaping mouth began to descend.

Nila howled when a brown and white Pitbull terrier landed on her back and bit savagely into her neck. With a growl of rage and pain, she reared and the dog slid off. Undeterred, it savaged her leg. She twisted, swept a huge, clawed hand at the dog, and hurled it several feet away.

She hadn't lost sight of her goal and shook herself, focused, and crept toward Marcel again. A small, black cat leapt over the quivering puppy, landed on her face, and scratched at her eyes. She howled again and tried to swipe it away, but it was too fast and scampered clear before she could reach it. Nila shook her head but before she could continue, the cat repeated its attack on her face and eyes with its claws. She snapped at it and tried to gore it with her antlers while she screamed in frustration.

Marcel squealed and continued to try to scramble away. The Pitbull ran around Nila and the cat and approached the puppy from the rear. She lifted him in her mouth by the scruff of his neck and raced toward the house. Without looking back, she ran down the emergency exit stairs and put the puppy down before she turned and scratched at the door.

***

The warmth from Scott's hand's radiated into Anne's knee and relieved the arthritic pain in the joint. "How does it feel?"

She flexed it. "That's wonderful. I wish you had time to do the other one."

He smiled. "We still have fifteen minutes. I can work on your wrists too."

"No, it's all right. I need to get out of the way before it all goes crazy down here. And you need to get that door."

Scott narrowed his eyes at her. He walked to the door, opened it, and peered into the hallway. "There's no one there."

"No, but it needed to be open or you wouldn't have heard the noise until it was too late." She smiled and patted his hand. "Thank you, young man. Don't forget to remove all the bracelets or it'll be a bloodbath around here."

He frowned and turned to the hallway again. "Can you hear that?" He stepped out, listened, and began to walk down the hallway, then paused at the intersection.

The old woman followed and turned toward the elevator. She pressed the call button and turned to him. "Chop, chop. And don't forget, curiosity killed the cat."

She stepped into the elevator, muttering, "Good heavens. You'd think they had all the time in the world."

Scott followed the sound of scratching. He moved more quickly when the howling started, pushed the bar, opened the fire door, and stared at the brown and white Pitbull. "Phyllis? You weren't supposed to go—"

Phyllis picked Marcel's drooping form up and raced inside as though something was chasing them.

He stood at the open doorway and wondered if he should take a look outside.

Curiosity killed the cat.

Quickly, he shut the door.

The sorcerer followed the dogs into the physio room and lifted Marcel onto the table. He untangled the cord with the whistle on it from the puppy's neck and feet, held the cord, and examined the whistle. It was easily recognizable as Nila's. He tried to touch it and it sparked. "Ow!" He dropped it.

When he glanced at Phyllis, she had shifted to human form. She had some bruising on her face and looked dazed. "Let me—"

"Fix the puppy. He's in a worse condition than me. I think his hind leg is broken."

Scott turned to Marcel, ran a hand over his hind leg, and muttered softly.

The dog whined.

"Marcel?" Dick called from the hallway.

"He's in here," he shouted in response.

The vampire appeared at the door. "I've been all over the place looking for him."

He looked grimly around the room and took everything in.

His eyes rested on Marcel and his face hardened. "What happened?"

"It was a wendigo," Phyllis answered. "I think it was Nila and I think she intended to eat him."

"I will kill her." His face was rigid and white with fury.

Marcel sat, whined, and barked at his voice and he stepped across to him, lifted the puppy, and let him lick his face. "Will Daddy kill the nasty wendigo, Marcel? Will he? Yes, he will." He looked at Scott. "That explains her breath."

The sorcerer frowned. "Why would she suddenly go nuts like that?"

"She caught me kissing Lexi and lost her—"

"Wait, what?"

"Keep up, Scott. Lexi and I are getting married and we want to adopt you."

"I thought you were Shaun," Phyllis interjected, her expression bewildered. "And who's Lexi?"

"I am. What's going on? She stood in the doorway.

Dick turned to her "Nila's a wendigo."

She stared at him, completely unsurprised. "That makes more sense than anything else in my life right now."

"It seems Nila was getting ready to eat Marcel but Phyllis saved him," Scott explained.

Dick inclined his head to Phyllis.

She waved him off. "I wouldn't have rescued him from her if it hadn't been for that cat."

After a momentary pause, the three of them asked, "Cat?"

"A black cat came from nowhere and attacked her face. It distracted her long enough for us to get away. That poor cat. I hope its luck didn't run out. I saw it go flying a couple of times."

Lexi was about to race down the hallway, then hesitated and turned to the old woman. "Where? Can you show me?"

Dick gaped at her. "With a wendigo on the loose? There could be a bloodbath."

Scott froze and stared at him.

He froze too. "What?"

The young man stared at his bracelet. "That's what Anne said. Remove the bracelets or there'll be a bloodbath."

The vampire stuck his arm out. "Off, please."

The sorcerer flicked the box open, retrieved the Graston tool, and struck the band lightly. A moment later, it was off.

Phyllis stood. "Okay, I'll take you out there." She shifted and led her along the hall to the exit door.

Lexi opened the door and the Pitbull went through. They raced across the lawn and she waited impatiently while Phyllis sniffed the ground.

After a moment, the old woman shifted again. "It was here. I smell wendigo and look, Nila's shredded clothes are everywhere. But I can't smell a cat. I smell something demonic, other than you. There's wendigo blood here. The trail heads into the trees. Do you want me to follow it?"

She shook her head. "No. Let's get to the house in case she's doubled back. I don't want to spend the night out here if she's roaming the hallways."

The old woman sighed.

Lexi looked at her. "Are you okay?"

"We won't find my friends, will we? Wendigos eat human

flesh and they eat once a week." Her eyes glittered with tears in the moonlight.

She hadn't put that together and was too startled to think about how to respond. Maisie and the others hadn't been moved out by Kindred. Nila had taken them. "I assumed Nila was Kindred because she arrived after the takeover. I bet she was placed here by Caleb."

They headed to the house in silence. Before they entered, she turned to Phyllis. "I know you prefer to keep your bracelet on but—"

"You can forget the bracelet. I have a houseful of friends to protect." The old woman strode in.

Lexi smiled and followed. She found Scott in the lobby and looked at the reception desk. "Where are the three amigos?"

"Still getting baked in the greenhouse."

She shook her head. "Let's go talk to them."

They headed to the greenhouse in the garden. She opened the door and waved a hand to clear the smoke from her face. "It's like a jazz club in here."

The three satyrs shushed each other repeatedly, the admonitions almost louder than their conversation.

When the two friends walked around a wall of moss, Stuart, Raj, and Josh sprawled on beanbags, frozen in the process of passing a bong, and looked at them with wide eyes.

Stuart flailed a hand as if in protest. "How did you find us?"

The sorcerer looked around. "You're not exactly well hidden."

Raj giggled.

Lexi made a mental eye-roll. "And we followed the smell."

The clerk's face went slack but brightened quickly. "We're looking for the dog."

Scott folded his arms. "How's that working out?"

"He hasn't come here yet, but we've set a trap." Stuart pointed to a sausage on the floor between them.

Lexi looked at Josh, who was poking himself in the cheek. "What's up with you?"

"I can't feel my face."

She shook her head. "Scott."

"On it. Sorry, boys." He muttered a few words and the satyrs blinked and shook their heads.

Raj looked at him. "Why did you do that, man?"

Josh pointed at Scott's arm. "Who removed your bracelet?"

Stuart slumped. "I did."

Raj looked at his colleague. "Why did you do that, man?"

Lexi had heard enough. "Okay, focus. Did any of you know that Nila's a wendigo?"

Stuart's face seemed expressive of an a-ha moment. "That makes so much sense."

Raj nodded. "Right?"

The three of them nodded at each other.

Lexi turned to her friend. "Are you sure you sobered them up completely?"

Scott shrugged. "I thought I had."

She looked at the three goat-legged men. "Okay, I'll try again. Nila's a wendigo and she's eaten three of the residents in the last month. She's loose on the grounds somewhere. Get your asses inside and protect the residents."

Stuart climbed off his beanbag. "Protect them? How? How do you even kill a wendigo?"

They stared at her.

"Fire." She turned to leave, then looked over her shoulder. "Or tear it to pieces."

She and Scott walked a few steps but stopped when they realized the satyrs weren't following.

Raj was picking up the beanbags and looking underneath. "Who's got the M&Ms?" He dipped a hand into a giant plant pot. "Never mind, I found them."

Lexi pinched the bridge of her nose while the satyrs filed out with their giant bag of peanut butter M&Ms.

Scott sent Raj to the third story of the building where the men's rooms were, and Josh sat on a chair in the hallway of the second story, the women's level. Stuart remained at his desk in the lobby but locked the doors. All three had armed themselves with a can of hairspray and a cigarette lighter.

They spent the night patrolling the building, checking windows and doors, and making sure Nila hadn't found her way back in.

Lexi walked into the staff kitchen. Her eyes were tired and gritty and she looked at Dick seated on a chair next to Marcel. "Shouldn't you be hiding in your room?"

He shrugged. "What's the point? Nila seems to have gone. I'm sorry if we kept you awake last night."

She laughed. "You mean after I went to bed two hours ago at five am? You didn't keep me awake. I didn't hear a thing."

"Really? Marcel howled in his sleep at one point. I would have thought someone on the other side of the wall would have heard him. The poor little thing."

With a frown, she looked at the wall. "I think the stairway's on the other side."

Dick raised an eyebrow. "No, that sweeps down the other way."

Mentally, she traced her steps through the house. "The hallway?"

He shook his head, bewildered. "It must be. This place is a labyrinth."

She rubbed her face. "I wonder where Limpet is."

The vampire looked a little sheepish. "I'm sorry I was horrible to him. If he hadn't attacked Nila, Marcel would be dead now."

Without meeting her gaze, he continued to stroke Marcel absently and focused on the wall. Suddenly, he stood.

Lexi narrowed her eyes at him. "What?"

"I only…" He walked out of the room.

She leaned over to stroke the puppy. Dick returned a few minutes later and jerked his head toward the hallway. "Come see."

Curious, she followed him out. They walked along the hallway.

"Where would you say the kitchen ends?"

Frowning in thought, she looked toward the door they'd just walked through. "Around here."

They looked in closets along the wall but none were particularly deep. Then, the hallway turned to the right. They passed a stairway, walked around a few corners and back in the direction they'd come, and passed the little hallway to hers and Scott's rooms in the turret.

When they reached the kitchen again, Scott was there trying to tempt Marcel with a chicken drumstick. He looked up. "I wondered where you'd gone."

Dick stared at him. "What are you doing?"

"I'm trying to cheer Marcel up. He looks sad."

The vampire looked at Marcel. "Scott. Come with us and bring Marcel. I don't want to leave him alone if he's awake. He might get frightened."

He followed them around the upper hallways. This time, they opened every single door and searched along every wall and in every cupboard.

Back in the kitchen, the sorcerer turned to the others. "So there's been a secret room on this floor, right under our noses all this time and we didn't realize it."

Dick looked ready to kick himself. "Because of the ridiculous design of the building."

"This explains why there are no windows in the rooms on this side of the hallway." Scott paused. "Just a minute." He left the room and Lexi followed him. He entered his bedroom, leaned out of the window, and sent one of his little mirror balls into the sky. Seconds later, it returned. Scott muttered a few words and the ball flattened to a wide disk. The two of them watched the journey the little sphere had taken over the roofs. A square section in stone blocks had been created in the middle of the tiled expanse, completely out of character with everything else.

"Let's go and take a look." He took her hand.

They appeared on the stone roof. It was roughly thirty feet in diameter.

Lexi looked for some way to enter the hidden room. "There's no roof access."

"I wonder what's in there." He apparated a little ball and dropped it, and it hovered for a few moments before it descended. It stopped on the roof and remained there.

She frowned at it. "What's it doing?"

"Nothing apparently." She looked irritated. "A magical field is keeping it out."

"Okay, let's get back to Dick." He took her hand again and they appeared in the kitchen.

The vampire looked up. "So what do you think the strange stone section is? It looks fairly old."

Scott narrowed his eyes. "How did you—"

Dick held his cell phone up. "Google Maps."

Lexi rolled her eyes. She was learning quickly how easy it was to rely on magic when other methods would suffice.

The sorcerer tried to direct his little ball through the wall. Initially, it sank through the stucco kitchen wall with no problem, but his frustrated face told her it hadn't breached the full wall.

He turned to Dick and put his hand out. "Can I look?"

The vampire held the phone out to him.

Scott looked for a few seconds, then handed it back. "Well,

what your app couldn't tell you is that there doesn't seem to be any way to get into that room. We've been all the way around it and found nothing. It must be magically sealed."

Dick gazed at the wall. "How thick would you say the walls are?"

He shrugged. "One and a half to two feet all the way around."

"And you believe that thickness of stone and the stone roof is simply sitting on a regular floor?"

They stared at him.

"It has to be a tower," he continued, "so it goes all the way down and the entrance must be on a lower level. This whole place has been built and designed to hide the existence of the tower in the middle."

Dick picked Marcel up and they headed down the stairs.

Once they understood that the convoluted design of the hallways was to draw attention away from the giant section in the middle of the building, it made much more sense.

Lexi stood outside a resident's room on the men's floor of the building. She chewed her lip in thought. "We can't simply start searching people's rooms while they're in them."

The vampire hesitated before he nodded. "Surely they'll go down for breakfast shortly anyway."

"They don't all go downstairs for breakfast. We need to get all the residents in one place so we can keep them safe and keep looking for a way into that tower."

They heard the elevator and as one, turned as the doors opened and Anne Lown shuffled out.

Scott hurried to her and offered his arm. "Anne. What are you doing up here?"

"Don't worry. I'm heading down again." She stepped past him and drew her arm back to punch the fire alarm on the wall. The glass broke and she yanked the handle down. The siren began to wail.

"Ouch." Anne shook her hand out, turned to Dick, and put her arms out for Marcel. He paused for a moment, then passed the puppy to her. She shuffled into the elevator.

"You're not supposed to use the elevator during a fire emergency," he called.

She flipped the bird as the doors closed.

"I like her," Scott yelled over the alarm.

The vampire nodded. "And that will do nicely." He walked along the hallway shouting, "Proceed slowly and carefully to the Fire Test Assembly Point which is the entertainment lounge. If you need help, press your call light and someone will come to you."

A man wandered out in his pajamas. "What's going on?"

"Fire alarm test," Lexi explained glibly.

"At this hour? I was napping."

"You're always napping." Raj wandered along the hallway with Josh and Stuart behind him.

"What's happening now?" the clerk asked.

"We're getting everyone into one place so they're easier to protect," Dick told them.

Stuart's eyes widened when he saw the vampire. "Dude. What are you doing out of the basement?" He halted in total shock when he realized the vampire was bathed in the morning light coming through a window.

He smirked and smoothed an eyebrow. "I've had a relapse."

People filed out of the rooms and they continued to direct them down.

"I can't get down those stairs," someone shouted.

"It's a test," Stuart called in response. "We're allowed to use the elevators. Those of you who can use the stairs follow Raj to—" He looked at Lexi.

"The entertainment lounge."

"Did you hear that? The entertainment lounge. If you need to use the elevator, line up here."

Albert stepped out of his room. "Why is this happening?"

Dick sighed. "I'm sorry. Kindred told us to do it. You know what total bastards they are."

"Oh, don't talk to me about those shit-heads." A man in a dressing gown wandered past with a walking stick.

Lexi chuckled. *Blame Kindred, why not?*

Stuart tapped her on the shoulder. "Has anyone seen Nila?"

She shook her head and turned to Scott. "You help Stuart get people out of their rooms. How will I know if there's an entrance?"

He fumbled in the bag on his back and pulled her pendant out, held it for a moment and muttered, then passed it to her. "If you come across anything hidden by magic, this will glow."

"You come with me," she told Josh.

The two of them went to the women's level where Anne and Phyllis were helping ladies out of their rooms.

"If you can manage the stairs," Josh shouted, "follow me to the entertainment lounge."

Scott's voice blared throughout the building as though he had a megaphone. "Please make your way to the entertainment lounge in your most expedient manner."

Lexi began to go through the rooms. She waved the pendant along the walls of every room but couldn't find anything that seemed suspicious.

She returned into the hallway, where Anne sat in her wheel-chair with Marcel in her hands. "Do you want help to get down-stairs, Anne?"

"Yes, please." She went with her in the elevator.

Only ten minutes had passed but all residents were gathered in the entertainment lounge.

Stuart approached her. "There are no kitchen staff."

Lexi frowned. "What time do they usually arrive?"

"An hour ago. And none of the day staff have arrived."

"Is that unusual?"

"It's unheard of."

She stepped out and found Dick about to enter the room. "It looks like all the staff have been canceled for today. Why would that be?"

He narrowed his eyes. "I think whatever they have planned will happen today. You keep searching. I'll distract the residents."

The vampire entered the room where most were still agreeing that Kindred were bastards. Some who hadn't seen him were wide-eyed. "Yes, I walk in the daylight. It's a thing. Since we're all here, let's have a sing-song." He walked to the piano, cracked his knuckles, and began to play "I get no kick from champagne."

Lexi stopped at the door and listened for a moment before she chuckled and shook her head and returned to the ladies' floor to check rooms and closets. She opened a door to find a lady fast asleep—Delia, according to the name on the door.

Quietly, she stepped in and checked the back wall of the room and the closet for any sign of an entrance to the tower.

"What are you doing?"

When she turned, the woman was seated in the bed. "I'm so sorry to disturb you. This is a shake-down."

Delia put her glasses on. "A what?"

"Kindred have insisted we check for drugs and associated paraphernalia."

"But I keep my medications in this drawer." The woman patted the bedside cupboard.

Lexi shook her head. "I'm looking for illegal drugs. You know, bennies, coke, smack, crack, meth, mollies, oxies, purple…drank."

The woman shook her fist at her. "They're not taking my oxies. Kindred are bastards"

"That does seem to be the consensus. If you have a prescription for them, you're fine. Well, you're clean. There's a fire test going on. Everyone's in the lounge."

"Good." She lay down, muttering under her breath.

Relieved that it hadn't proved too much of a problem, she

stepped into the hallway but wasn't sure what to do about the woman.

Scott leaned against the wall and grinned. "Purple drank? Where did you get all that?"

"Isaac used to listen to a ton of rap music. Have you finished upstairs already?"

He nodded. "Stuart and Raj helped with the residents."

"This woman doesn't want to budge. I don't want to leave her alone with a wendigo on the loose."

"A what?" Delia stepped out. "Did you say a wendigo?"

"Well—"

The woman scuttled down the hallway like she might once have been an Olympic sprinter.

Scott watched her with a grin. "That's solved that problem."

They finished searching the rest of the rooms on that level and continued while they listened to Dick belting out "My Kind of Town."

They found Delia in the lobby, trying to take her bracelet off with a pair of toenail clippers.

The sorcerer leaned over the front desk as they walked past and snaffled the tuning fork. "I'll sort that out for you."

Dick noticed them as they entered the room. "Okay, ladies and gentlemen. Let's have a little chat, shall we?"

The residents booed.

Patrick stepped onto the stage. "Hold up now. Something's been going on here that everyone needs to know. We've all been concerned about our friends going missing. Well, now I have answers." He drew a deep breath. "Nila is a wendigo."

Phyllis stood beside him. "I can confirm it. I saw her myself last night."

Someone shouted, "No one disbelieves you, Patrick."

"That explains her breath," another resident muttered.

Scott moved to the front. "I know some of you might be nervous about the idea of removing your bracelets—"

"Get these damn things off and let us protect ourselves," a man shouted.

Patrick leaned closer and added quietly. "Except Albert. He's crazy."

The sorcerer took the old man's arm and prepared to strike the bracelet with the tuning fork. The satyrs arranged themselves around Albert.

The moment he struck the band, it fell. Scott muttered and the note lingered and grew louder. The sound of bracelets falling jangled around the room.

Stuart caught Albert's bracelet in mid-air and snapped it onto him again. The crazy old man looked sadly at it.

"What now?" Patrick asked Lexi.

She frowned. "No day staff have arrived. You should get everyone into the kitchen and dining room and see if you can feed them."

He looked at all the people with their abilities returned. Some were shifting but others weren't. "They'd only not plan to feed us if they thought we wouldn't be here to need feeding."

"That was our thought. Barricade yourselves in." She turned to the satyrs. "Can you go in with them? Look after them?"

Stuart nodded.

When the residents had been herded into the dining room, Lexi, Scott, and Dick continued with their search.

They worked their way around the tower's walls but found nothing.

She wasn't to be deterred. "Okay. Basement."

CHAPTER NINETEEN

They trudged down the stairs to the basement, checked all the rooms, and met at the bottom of the stairs again.

"Nothing. What's the point of leaving that tower in the middle of the building?" Lexi turned to the painting. "I don't suppose you'd care to give up your secrets, would you, Mr. Maybury?"

She froze as she remembered something. Her gaze slid to the closet she'd hidden in. "Oh, for God's sake." She went to the door, yanked it open, and found the wooden stick she'd picked up when she had hidden from Nila. Looking around, she found a small slot on the floor beside the wall. She put the stick into the hole, pulled, and looked around inside the closet. "Dammit. It must be something else."

"Er...Lexi." Dick called.

Hastily, she stepped out. The inset wall with the picture had swung upward to reveal a staircase leading down.

The sorcerer shook his head. "I've been all over this place feeling for some kind of magical spell. I can't believe it was a common hidden door."

Lexi moved toward the entrance.

"Wait," Scott whispered.

When she turned, he held her katana out. She took it and nodded.

They entered the old stone tower. The steps opened into a wide empty room, with a curved staircase leading up along the wall. They spread out. Although the space was dark, a flicker of light indicated that the room above was lit with torches. The only other light was from the doorway they had entered through.

Strange markings covered the walls but were most clearly visible where the light from the doorway bounced off the opposite wall. Lexi moved slowly toward it to see if she could work out what the symbols were. As she gazed at the markings, a shadow appeared across them in the shape of a head with antlers.

She spun and swung her katana into Nila's impossibly strong antlers. Vibrations reverberated along the blade to the handle but left not even a dent in her target.

"Good Lord, what a smell." Dick stood to the side and waved his hand in front of his face.

The wendigo turned to him and snarled. Drool dripped from her mouth and her claws dragged loudly along the stone.

"I'm sorry dearest," he continued. "It really would never have worked between us. And the fact that you're a stinking, drooling monster isn't even the number one reason."

Nila howled and stepped toward him. Lexi glanced at the stairs to the next floor but she didn't dare to take her focus off their adversary.

Dick noticed her indecision. "Off you go, you two. I'll keep her busy."

Her screech reverberated in the wide chamber as she attacked with her head lowered. Dick evaded easily at vamp speed and she was infuriated.

A sound from the doorway drew her attention. A pack of wolves, foxes, dogs, and bears crowded into the room. They snapped and snarled at Nila, led by a brown and white Pitbull who jerked her head at Lexi to tell her to move along.

She and Scott headed to the next level as the pack encircled the wendigo.

Ever cautious, she kept her back to the outer wall of the tower as they climbed the stairs into the next room. It was empty except for two shapes on the floor which were clearly bodies. She ran to one. It was Bryan.

Scott crouched beside him and checked his vitals. "He seems perfectly healthy but I don't see any brain function." He put his hand onto the man's head and closed his eyes. "There doesn't seem to be a reason for his condition but it's like his mind is empty."

Lexi approached the second body. It was an old lady who was very much alive but bound and shivering. "Are you Maisie?"

The woman nodded and she untied her. "Scott, blanket and water."

He retrieved both items from his bag and wrapped the blanket around the woman. She gulped the water thirstily.

"Don't leave me."

She put a finger to her lips and looked at Scott.

The sorcerer put a hand on the side of her head. "Sleep." The woman slipped into unconsciousness and he eased her down carefully and covered her.

They returned to Bryan and Lexi looked at him. "Could he have retreated into his dimensional pocket?"

Scott frowned in thought. "I suppose it's possible."

She nodded. "I'm going to see if I can get in there."

He shook his head. "I don't think that's a good idea. You might not be able to get in, and what if you do and can't get out again?"

"I have to try." Lexi put her hand onto Bryan's face, closed her eyes, and imagined where she wanted to be.

Once inside his closet, she stepped to the mirrored door and placed her hand on it. It swung open without a push and she walked to the edge of the platform over the big hall. The entire space was silent and nothing showed on the screens.

"Bryan?" There was no response so she took a deep breath and descended.

She went to the most recent booth and looked at the board with Caleb's name on it. There were no new updates but she touched the screen in the booth and it came to life.

The sorcerer stared out of the screen. "Calm down, Bryan. I won't kill you. Not your body, anyway. When Azatoth possesses Alicia, he will have his powers and he'll have access to her legacy abilities, which now include her sister's. With you alive, he'll also have your magic through the blood match. He will be the most powerful being in existence. I would have liked that to have been me, but it wasn't to be."

Aghast, she watched the scene play out.

Why isn't Bryan fighting this?

"I know," Caleb continued, "you're terrified that you'll be frozen inside your own body forever. But it won't be like that. I wouldn't do that to you. I'm not a monster. You won't be in there. You'll merely be a power source, nothing more."

The man stretched his hand to Bryan and the screen went blank.

Lexi looked around. She knew it was time to leave. He was gone. But still, she wondered why all this was still there if he had been erased.

She walked through the aisles to the black door with *Bad Stuff* written on it, put her hand on it, took a breath, and opened it.

This was a room with a few aisles. She saw pictures of herself from his perspective. One revealed the moment she was dragged away screaming before he was tranquilized and removed from the Braxton family at fifteen.

In the next booth, she found where he and Alicia had argued. He had shifted and clawed her face. She closed her eyes. What a burden to have to live with.

"Hello, Lexi-Loo."

Startled, she spun toward his voice. Bryan sat inside a cell. "Bryan! Did Caleb put you in here?"

He stood and walked to the bars. "No, I did."

Lexi walked closer. This Bryan seemed younger than the body he inhabited. "I don't understand."

"I've been in here since that happened." He indicated the video she'd just watched of when he'd slashed Alicia's face.

Her jaw dropped. "But that must have been five years ago."

"I separated the wolf from the rest of me and left it in here. I'm the part of me that did that. I'm the wolf."

"But you're not a wolf."

"I'm a were, not a shifter. We only change on a full moon, remember? Unless commanded by an alpha, which I don't have."

She was horrified. "You've been trapped inside a cell within your mind for this long?"

Bryan looked at her for a long moment, then lowered his gaze. "She's worth it. I love her and I had to keep her safe."

In that moment, she realized what had seemed wrong with him. He didn't have the warmth or the passion of the Bryan she'd known all those years ago. She had assumed he had grown out of those traits, but the truth was that he'd locked them away.

He looked at her now, his face puzzled. "Why are you here?"

"Caleb has taken Alicia and he's done something to you. You're not responsive. The rest of your awareness… I think it's gone for good."

"There's nothing I can do about that. I felt the other part had gone but being in here, I had no idea what had happened." He shrugged.

Lexi put her hands on the bars. "Your body is lying there. We have to get Alicia back so we need to get you out of here."

"Leave me here. I couldn't bear to hurt you too." He put a hand over hers. "You were my first love, do you know that?"

"Of course I do." She put a hand over his.

Bryan's face showed a whole range of emotions but mostly, he looked wretched. "You have to leave me here."

She yanked her hands away and looked for the door. There wasn't one. "The hell I do. You have to man up and get out of here. This body currently has no one at the wheel. You need to step up."

"But what if I hurt someone?"

"If you do nothing, you'll hurt many more people. Caleb and his demon pal will use your blood match with Alicia to hurt others. As you've already pointed out, you're a were. You change at the full moon and this is not a full moon. Alicia needs your help. You said you loved her. It's time to prove it."

Frustrated, she swung her katana against the cage but nothing happened beyond a loud ringing.

"That's the other problem. I was worried I'd weaken and escape. No known weapon or magic can release me." He shrugged.

"No known magic?" She stared at her katana and watched as the blade transformed to a dark hematite that glittered with flashes of yellow light.

She looked at him.

He stepped back in shock. "Your eyes—"

"Stand farther back. I'm not sure how this will work." She swung the blade at the bars and the cage burst open. In the next moment, she was in the tower with Scott.

Bryan lay motionless for a moment before he shook his head and groaned. He sat and looked at his hands, turning and flexing them in something close to wonder. "I forgot what a real body feels like." He looked at Scott with a puzzled expression, then shook his head as though to slough off a deep sleep. "That's so much to take in at once. Hi, Scott."

Lexi realized he must be receiving five years of updates from his dimensional pocket.

He stood and held a hand out, and an energy ball appeared and disappeared. He looked at her and nodded.

Dick appeared. "It's not going well down there. She's gored a dozen of the shifters." He looked at a gash across his chest that was healing as he spoke. "And me. She gored me and I don't even want to think about what this shirt cost."

Scott turned to him. "I'll come with you. You two keep going." He disappeared.

She didn't like being separated from him but he'd made the call and left. Rather than follow him, she nodded to Dick who disappeared at vamp speed.

Lexi and Bryan moved up to the next level.

Caleb stood with his back to them and Alicia lay on a wooden altar.

From her position on the stairs, she could see that her sister was shiny, no doubt covered in the stinking grease they'd used on the demon. She realized it must be needed for the ritual. What they now tried to do with Alicia, they'd probably already tried and failed with the demon.

The sorcerer was drawing a large rectangle like a doorway on the wall with a lump of brimstone. A squeak drew her attention to a box at his feet. It was Limpet, caged again, and he looked fearfully at her.

She glanced at Bryan, whose gaze was fixed on his wife. Calmly, she put a hand on his arm to get his attention. She signaled that he should get to Alicia and translocate them both away while she would deal with Caleb. He nodded. They stepped into the room and froze.

The man turned. He looked at Bryan, obviously shocked. "Well, I'm not sure how you achieved that, but kudos."

Lexi tried to open her mouth but couldn't manage it. A slight swivel of her eyes was all she could do.

"I'm afraid you've stumbled into my little safe space." He looked at Bryan. "You can't access your magic." His gaze shifted to her. "Or move. I certainly learned my lesson after our last encounter, although I understand you're not quite as formidable as you once were."

She tried to access her magic but found nothing.

Caleb finished drawing his portal and turned to her. "Are you surprised that I considered you a formidable opponent? I know you thought yourself defective, but you have a keen mind and excellent skills. Many of your contemporaries are lazy. They rely on the legacy enhancements or the magic from their mage. But you, Miss Braxton, are the product of your own will and determination. You've been mentioned in the council several times over the years."

There was a tiny part of her that couldn't stop herself from feeling proud. Her pride annoyed her, though.

"I wanted to experiment with the two of you," their adversary continued, "but your mother would never allow it."

Had Lexi not already been frozen, his casual mention of her mother would have chilled her to the bone. She wanted to rip the truth from him, but all she could do was listen.

"I wonder if it would have made any difference had you gained all the legacy abilities and become Azatoth's host. Well, it's too late to change plans at this late stage. Your sister is ready."

Caleb walked to the woman who lay unconscious on the altar. He picked a knife up and held it over her. "I'm afraid all you've been able to achieve is a ringside seat. Still, I'm sure it'll be quite a show." He cut Alicia's arm and allowed her blood to run into a bowl.

Lexi's eyes couldn't even widen.

Carefully, he ran a finger over the cut and healed it. "I mustn't damage the goods." He placed her arm down and stood staring at her. After a long moment, he reached a finger to her face and brushed it softly across her lips. Looking at Lexi, he smiled and licked his lips.

She wondered what would happen if she vomited in this paralyzed state.

He walked to the wall, dipped his fingers into the bowl, and drew an intricate design on the wall in the blood. That done, he crouched beside the box at his feet, unlatched it, and took Limpet out. "Azatoth is ready now." He looked at Lexi again. "This is all your fault, you know. If you hadn't interfered with him coming through the true portal in his own body, we wouldn't have to thin the veil and allow his essence to assume control of poor Alicia. It is such a shame. And if you'd stayed away from Alicia, you wouldn't have made her a viable host for him. You did that. I suppose we should thank you. I'm sure Azatoth will find a way. He is so creative."

A guttural scream issued from a lower level of the tower and Caleb sighed. "Poor Nila. She was very loyal. Azatoth liked her. He'll be vexed."

Scott and Dick appeared beside her and were instantly frozen.

"Ah, if it isn't my old friend William Levin. I do hope we have some time to chat later. I appear to be unable to find Betsy and Todd. I think you might be able to help with that." The evil sorcerer turned and tightened his grasp on Limpet. The little demon howled but he held the creature against the wall, which began to undulate.

Lexi stared helplessly as the barrier began to fade when the veil thinned.

The shape of a huge creature became visible. It wasn't as clear as the portal in Palm Springs but she could see Azatoth's outline.

Terror crept into her frozen bones. She was aware that Alicia stirred. This monster would kill them all, probably in the body of her sister, and she was powerless to prevent it.

Limpet struggled in his captor's hand. He freed an arm, plunged it into the wall, and almost made a tiny hole in the veil.

Caleb tightened his grip. "You're going nowhere."

The little demon relaxed in his hand as the veil thinned. Lexi noticed that Limpet pushed his arm slowly deeper into the wall.

She knew the exact moment when the veil was breached, even though the hole was no thicker than Limpet's skinny little arm. She felt the source of her power as it flooded the room and crept into her body, infused her bones, and released her from the paralysis. Her brimstone ring began to glow, and her unhealing scar tickled as energy surged through it. She closed her eyes and when she opened them again, they were black.

Caleb's gaze remained fixed on the Azatoth's silhouette, which became slightly more defined as the veil continued to thin.

Lexi turned to Scott as she moved silently past him. She allowed herself a tiny smile at Dick.

Her adversary must have sensed when she was directly behind him. He spun with a look of shock on his face. "How—"

He began to bring his arm away from the wall but she twisted it back so violently, a bone in his arm snapped. He screamed and fell to his knees. She put her hand onto Limpet to ensure that the wall remained in a state of flux. When she kicked Caleb in the temple, he went out like a light. Azatoth moved closer to the veil. His great arms came up and pounded against it.

She dropped her katana and it stuck into the floorboard and wobbled at her side. Her expression grim, she turned to the massive demon, made a fist, and punched her arm through the veil. It was like driving a blow through ballistics gel. She struck his rib cage and when her fist breached it, she grasped his heart and ripped it from his chest.

The faded figure of the large demon crumpled. Lexi yanked her arm away. Her hand was covered in dark-red, almost black blood. She crushed the heart and dropped the sticky mess onto the floor. Limpet withdrew from the wall and she allowed him to run up her arm and scamper to the floor.

When she turned, the others were still frozen.

Caleb began to stir. He opened his eyes and squinted as she retrieved her katana.

He cradled his broken arm and touched his head. "He's gone. He's finally gone." He was sobbing. "You've freed me. Thank you."

Lexi stared at him, unmoved. "You're welcome."

"He's been controlling me." The man looked down and flinched when Limpet jumped onto his knee and scuttled up his arm and onto his shoulder. He turned to her. "All these years, I thought there was no escape." He clutched his arm and winced.

She raised an eyebrow. "I know you've already healed it."

He paused and seemed to weigh his options. "Ah! I see. Then you should probably look at your friends. I can squeeze the life out of them from here so you might want to say goodbye."

While he spoke, Limpet sat on his shoulders. He dropped his head back to allow it to grow and his mouth to widen.

"Who would you like me to kill first? Your sister? You don't even know her. Or William—he's had a hundred years already. I could get rid of Scott for you and you could be with Bryan like you were always meant to be."

Limpet brought his head forward at incredible speed, and the sorcerer's entire skull was engulfed by his mouth. One loud crunch later, the headless body sagged and remained unmoving.

When Caleb's hold over the others broke, Bryan rushed to Alicia, Scott ran to Lexi's side, and Dick simply stood and stared at Lexi while he pointed at Limpet. "I told you. I fucking told you."

Lexi crept through the darkened hallway and tiptoed past ladders and dust sheets. The smell of fresh paint was evident but it wasn't unpleasant. Silently, she opened the door and approached the bed. She extended her hand tentatively to touch the sleeper's shoulder but the woman's eyes jerked open and looked directly at her.

"How are we doing?" she whispered

Anne Lown pushed her covers aside to reveal that she was fully dressed. She gave her a thumbs-up. "On track."

She helped the old lady out of bed. The woman retrieved her purse and walked past her wheelchair. She hadn't needed it since Scott had given her a full physio session.

Quickly, she headed into the room opposite hers and Lexi went to Phyllis' room. The door opened as she approached it and Phyllis walked out with Patrick behind her.

"Phyllis!" She smirked. "I'm sure that's against the rules."

"A little anarchy never hurt anyone." The old woman winked, and Patrick blushed.

"What's going on?" A loud voice made her jump.

Lexi turned as Stuart walked toward her on his goat legs. His eyes were so wide they looked like Limpet's.

He's baked again.

"This is a break-out," she explained,

His jaw dropped. "But you can't. I'll have to call Erika."

After the former physio had recently come into some money, she bought Emmersley for a steal at two million dollars and was putting additional funds into smartening it up.

She smirked. "Yes, you should do that. I think she should know that you three are getting high in the greenhouse every night."

Stuart froze. His gaze darted around for a few seconds. "You're bringing everyone back though, right?"

"Sure. We're only taking them for a night out."

He chewed his lip. "Where are you all going?"

"Vegas."

His face brightened. "Oh, wow! Can I come?"

An object hurtled seemingly out of nowhere and caught him between the eyes. It burst and he fell and immediately started snoring.

Lexi turned to the ladies, who had all exited their rooms and were waiting, dressed and ready for their adventure. "Who was that?"

"Sorry," said a little voice from the back of the hallway.

She grinned. "Nice shot. I need to check on the guys." She translocated and appeared next to Scott.

He jumped. "Jesus, can you not do that? Announce yourself."

Her chuckle drew one in response. She looked along the hallway filled with elderly men and turned to him. "Good to go?"

A grumpy voice down the hall shouted, "Just hurry up. I need to pee."

Scott's cell appeared in his hand and he sent a text.

The fae door appeared and Dolores walked through.

"Are you sure this will work?" Lexi whispered.

Her boss opened her hand to reveal the talisman." This will get us into Vegas but the wards are up again. Dick's rented a bus to take us out of town for the journey back." She turned to the men. "Okay, let's move."

As they filed through the fae door, Lexi vanished and returned to the ladies. "All right, girls, our ride's coming."

Dolores appeared with the door and the women chattered excitedly as they walked through.

Lexi looked at Stuart who was still asleep on the floor but now, he was covered in grass and daisies. It was very pretty. She and Dolores walked through the portal to New York, New York in Las Vegas. The vampire and Marcel waited for them beside Albin. Dick cut his gaze to the historian and back to her and wiggled his eyebrows. He looked like the cat that got the cream.

"Where's Scott?" she asked.

He glanced around. "I don't know. He came through. I saw him."

She wandered around the casino floor for a while and smiled at Albert, who had filled his pockets with quarters. "Keep your pants on, Albert, or you'll lose your money."

When she couldn't locate her friend visually, she took her silver teardrop pendant out and held it tightly in her hand. "Come on, where is he?"

Its gentle pull guided her through the building and the Big Apple Arcade to where Scott waited in a line for the rollercoaster.

He grinned. "Great! Are you all coming on?"

Lexi turned. She seemed to have unwittingly led the whole group to the arcade. "Not me." She held her hands up. "Maybe later." She pulled her cell out and sent a text.

Phyllis, Anne, and Patrick joined the line behind him while the others crowded around the arcade games.

When his turn finally came, Scott scrambled excitedly into the car and secured himself. He seemed barely able to move an inch.

Anne Lown, seated beside him, frowned. "I'm sorry. This will end badly for you."

Patrick turned in the seat in front. "Don't be such a Debbie Downer." He was spun and wrenched into his seat by a young woman who secured him. "I'm beginning to regret this myself."

"Don't be scared, Patrick. I'll protect you." Phyllis squeezed his knee.

A whistle blew and Lexi chuckled at the barrier as they all flinched visibly at the sound. The car jerked to a start on the roller coaster and the moment was forgotten. Scott's dimple-popping grin appeared. *He still looks like a twelve-year-old.* She smiled.

She sensed rather than saw the woman approach.

Alicia leaned on the barrier next to her. "Bryan will be disappointed to have missed this."

"Oh?" She raised an eyebrow. "Where is he?"

"It's the first night of the full moon. He's in the bayou with Geraldine's pack. They're looking after him as he hasn't physically shifted for five years."

She looked at her sister's face. "You've hidden your scars."

Alicia touched her cheek. "They're gone now. I let him take them away."

Lexi pushed away from the barrier "Why did you wait so long to do that?"

"I was punishing him." The woman shrugged.

She raised an eyebrow. "For five years?"

"I was angry."

"For five years?" She raised both eyebrows.

Alicia laughed, then frowned. "I could feel his emotions through the link. He didn't seem bothered by what he'd done. I could have forgiven him for doing it but not for not caring. Of course, I know now that he'd imprisoned the wolf and his emotions along with it."

Lexi nodded. "How are you coping with the enhanced legacy abilities?"

"I feel fine now. Everything seems to have settled, but that's why I wanted to see you. If you want to try to take some of it back, you're welcome to." She held her hand out.

"I don't need to." She shook her head firmly. "I'm dealing with more than enough right now learning how to use and control this new ability."

Alicia bit her lip, then took a deep breath. "I'd feel happier if you tried. You're my sister and I want to know if it's safe to hug you."

She nodded, held her hand above her companion's, then lowered it and took her sister's hand. They looked pensively into each other's eyes.

"Anything?" Lexi asked.

Her twin drew the corners of her mouth down and shook her head. "Nope, you?"

With a small smile, she shook her head. "Not a thing."

Alicia laughed. "I guess that's it, then. You have what you were supposed to have, and I have what I was supposed to have." She narrowed her eyes. "It's so weird sensing the dark sorcery within you. It's similar to sensing a demon but not quite. I've never known anything like it."

"None of us have. Scott says there hasn't been a dark sorcerer for hundreds of years."

The woman slowly twirled a display carousel of Las Vegas magnets and keyrings. "Do you think you'll come back? To Kindred?"

She shook her head. "I don't think so. I still have too many unanswered questions."

"Bryan told me about the little boy, the sorcerer who was placed with your family."

Lexi sighed. She turned and they looked at the rollercoaster.

"There's that, but there are other things. Someone's been taking the wards down here in Vegas to commit crimes. Dolores says they're kept in place by joint spells between Kindred and the Fae Elders. Neither one can bring them down without the knowledge and support of the other. I guess it could have been Caleb's doing as head of the council, but he performed forbidden magic in a cabal of thirteen. That could have been the Kindred council themselves."

Alicia shrugged. "The Kindred council has denied any knowledge of his activities. They couldn't distance themselves from Emmersley fast enough. And they've started an investigation into some of the aliases he used. How will you know what's going on in Kindred if you avoid us?"

"And finally, there's our parents—our real parents." Lexi turned to her sister. "I want to know who they were or are. Do you know anything about them?"

"My earliest memories are of New Orleans. I don't remember having any other parents. I've been in Bryan's dimensional pocket. That's something else. He's shown me how to protect and conceal my memories."

Lexi felt embarrassed, knowing there were memories of her in there. She wondered if Alicia would have seen the memories she had seen, the posters and the books, but decided she wouldn't ask. It wasn't her business what he shared with his wife.

"Thank you for what you did for us. You saved our lives. So, I'll give you that hug now. I'm merely a Kindred-legacy-killing-machine sharing a hug with her ex-Kindred-legacy-killing-machine-turned-dark-sorcerer sister. There's nothing weird about that."

Her laugh was spontaneous. "When you put it like that, it all seems perfectly normal."

They hugged and while it did feel weird, it was a good weird.

When they drew apart, they stood side by side while she searched the screens for Scott's face on the roller coaster. As her eyes searched each frame, she continued the conversation. "I'm in touch with my unit now. They tell me Warren, Scott's rejected blood match, is still harassing them. He tried to force them to submit to Eric for a memory extraction so he could find out what they know. He seems to have found a soulmate in Eric and he's moved to Colorado to join his unit."

Alicia's jaw dropped. "I hope the council said no to that request."

"For now. But Caleb's gone and Eric's ambitious. There's an opening on the council and apparently, he's trying to slide into it."

Lexi smiled as her eyes found a hilarious photograph of Scott. *There he is.*

She stepped up to the counter and paid for the picture.

The door opened and he walked through, dripping wet and covered in a pink substance from his neck to his shoes. "Who takes a milkshake onto a rollercoaster? Seriously, who? And why does this always happen to me?"

Anne walked past. "I tried to warn you."

Lexi and Alicia laughed.

Dick and Albin walked Marcel along Las Vegas Boulevard. They watched the fountains at the Bellagio for a while, then continued to walk until they turned off the Strip to walk the few blocks to the condo.

The historian smiled. "So you're going to be staying for a while."

"Kindred will be all over Palm Springs for some time. I think it's best I stay out of the way. And I have the place here so why not?"

"Why not indeed."

"I won't be here all the time," he continued. "We'll still go wherever the work takes us, but it'll be nice to have a base here."

They stepped aside to allow a group of young men walking a rottweiler to pass.

One of them pointed at Marcel and laughed. "Titus could eat that little rat. Couldn't you, Titus?"

His friends began to mutter encouragement. "Sic him."

Albin raised an eyebrow. "I wouldn't threaten Marcel in front of him."

They looked at Dick. "What will you do about it?"

The vampire smoothed an eyebrow. "He's not talking about me. He means *him.*"

A black cat with impossibly large, amber, saucer-like eyes slunk out from the shadows and meowed. Its mouth seemed disquietingly wide with teeth that looked much too long. It strode forward in a not very cat-like fashion, stood between Marcel and Titus, and hissed. The large dog squealed and bolted down the street, dragging his owner behind him. The others followed.

Dick grinned. "Good boy, Limpet. Who's going to get a nice raw steak?"

The next morning, Lexi and Scott sat outside their condo. She gazed, mesmerized, into the sparkling depths of her unhealing scar. When she felt him looking at her, she glanced at him and smiled.

"Do you still need me as a partner?" he asked,

She had guessed the question would come. "Do you still need me? I don't know if I'm even a legacy anymore. Aren't I a sorcerer now?"

He shrugged. "If your sorcerer abilities did come through the legacy bloodline, then you're a legacy who favors that ability."

"But I thought sorcery wasn't genetic." She took a sip of her coffee.

"So did I. Maybe dark sorcery is different."

"Maybe I should go back to Kindred and train to be a mage."

Scott frowned. "I've thought about that."

"I was kidding."

"No, not about going back to Kindred. I've thought about what might happen if they find out what you are. I've read the history books. I don't think the dark sorcerers died off. They were killed off."

"Are you saying I'll have a price on my head?"

He shrugged and looked away, his expression uncertain. "Where does this leave us?

Lexi turned toward him. "I don't know whether we're still matched or not, but unless you have somewhere else you need to be, I hope you won't leave. I mean...I understand if you've decided—"

"No, I haven't. I want us to keep working together. You need to learn how to use your magic now." Scott dug in his bag and retrieved her pendant.

She narrowed her eyes. "How do you always get that back?"

He held the silver teardrop in his hand.

"Are you going to make me jewelry again? I'll be honest, I don't mind when you do that."

"I'm not. We are."

After a moment, she opened her hand and he dropped the teardrop into her palm. He held his hand over hers and closed his eyes. She felt his intention immediately. Her eyes snapped open. "Is our link back?"

Scott turned his mouth down. "No, this is how I learned to do some of my spells. A teacher and pupil aren't matched but there is a connection, a flow of understanding between them.

Lexi grinned. She'd missed her connection with Scott and this alternative might be enough. Pleased, she closed her eyes again. He showed her how to change the form of the metal and she decided on a shape. Her palm tickled as the metal shifted within it. He removed his hand and she looked at the metal that had darkened again to look like a shiny, dark metal oval-shaped hoop.

He picked it up. "Nice work." He stepped behind her and clicked the clasp closed.

Dick walked outside to where they sat drinking coffee.

"Good morning," he said cheerfully and sat.

She took a sip of coffee then turned her face to him. "We know. Thin walls remember?"

"Oops." Albin stepped out and stood behind the chair. He kissed the vampire on top of his head and sat beside him. "Did your friends get home safely?"

Scott nodded. "All present and correct."

Dick picked an envelope up and turned it in his hands. "This looks interesting."

Lexi slid her gaze to the side and smirked.

He opened the large envelope with *Dick* written on the front and pulled out a sheet of paper and a smaller envelope. "Oh, it's from Dolores." He unfolded the sheet and read the short note.

"Dear Dick, please find enclosed your new ID and associated documents." He looked at Albin. "How odd. I haven't decided on a new name yet." He looked at the note and continued. "The documents contain your new name as chosen by *Lexi*." He stared at her with a look of pure horror on his face. "Oh, dear God, not again. What now?"

Scott looked at her. "You didn't."

Her lip twitched.

The vampire tore the smaller envelope and retrieved the pass-port. "Dick Erwin." He looked at her. "I don't get it." He tried it slowly "Dick-Er-win." Then, still puzzled, he tried it fast. "Dickerwin."

Albin picked the new driving license up. "I think that's a German name."

Dick grabbed his cell phone and began to type furiously, then read out loud, "Eric, Ernst...here we are, Erwin in German means..." He looked at Lexi, who studied her nails.

Scott leaned forward. "Well?"

He swallowed. "Erwin...honored or trusted friend."

The sorcerer blew a sharp breath of relief. He looked at him. "Are you crying?"

"No. I'm allergic to...to... Oh, come here." The vampire hauled her out of her seat and hugged her.

She patted his back. "Stop that. You'll ruin my reputation as a kickass dark sorcerer."

I turned my attention to book 3 shortly after November 2019. I'd been motivated by the Vegas conference and threw myself straight into it. Of course, it needed a location to start it off and I was starting to feel that Lexi, Scott and Dick deserved a home; Somewhere they could stay that wasn't a flea-infested hovel. And with 20Books Vegas still clearly visible in my rear-view mirror, where else but there?

Michael and I knocked a few ideas around. He thought Dick was just too confident. He's got the looks, confidence, style, and money (FYI, this is Dick I'm describing, not Michael) but he was right. Dick needed a love interest who would keep him on his toes. And Marcel needed a little pal too. I think our strange little family is almost complete. Almost.

We continued to work on the book through into the new year while strange whispers began to travel around the world. By the time London Book Fair was due to take place in March, the world was shutting down. The book fair was cancelled but I attended another author conference in London anyway. Hey, while I'm talking about that conference, I just want to mention that Michael referred to me… while he was onstage…on video, and in front of an audience… as "PHENOMENAL." I just felt that was worth mentioning.

If you don't believe me, I've got it recorded on a loop. If you see me, just ask, I'll be delighted to play it for you. Absolutely bloody delighted.

Anyway, I then spent a few great days with Michael, Judith, Sarah Noffke, Andrew Dobell, and a bunch of other fabulous authors… And some of the greatest, most awesome superfans on earth. I'm so glad I went because that was pretty much the last time I went anywhere.

While I was in London, I finished this book and managed to get a "The End" photo with Michael.

https://www.bookbub.com/authors/michael-anderle